Adventures in Reading

Ruskin Bond is known for his signature simplistic and witty writing style. He is the author of several bestselling short stories, novellas, collections, essays and children's books; and has contributed a number of poems and articles to various magazines and anthologies. At the age of twenty-three, he won the prestigious John Llewellyn Rhys Prize for his first novel, *The Room on the Roof.* He was also the recipient of the Padma Shri in 1999, Lifetime Achievement Award by the Delhi Government in 2012 and the Padma Bhushan in 2014.

Born in 1934, Ruskin Bond grew up in Jamnagar, Shimla, New Delhi and Dehradun. Apart from three years in the UK, he has spent all his life in India, and now lives in Landour, Mussoorie, with his adopted family.

RUSKIN BOND

Adventures in Reading

RUPA

Published by
Rupa Publications India Pvt. Ltd 2022
7/16, Ansari Road, Daryaganj
New Delhi 110002

Sales centres:
Allahabad Bengaluru Chennai
Hyderabad Jaipur Kathmandu
Kolkata Mumbai

ISBN: 978-93-5520-403-5

First impression 2022

10 9 8 7 6 5 4 3 2 1

Moral right of the author has been asserted.

CONTENTS

INTRODUCTION

How many of us take even a few minutes out for ourselves, sit in solitude and look within? More importantly, how many of us understand how our pasts make us who we are today? Days, weeks and months go by us like the Mussoorie Express, and we are unable to find the time or the patience to ponder upon who we are, what makes us happy and what drives us to live on—what do our lives *really* mean? Amidst fast-paced routines and a heavy dependence on technology, it is quite easy for us to forget noticing all the beauty around us.

The reality is, we are often too focused on what lies ahead. Aren't a lot of us inclined towards only seeing the problems in our lives glaring at us like ugly monsters? We end up ignoring how far we have *already* come, having made our ways through the varying seasons of life, some sunny and rosy like spring, some harsh and bleak like wintertime. At times, we unknowingly overlook the tiny, day-to-day joys that make life worth living— the tinkering laughter of a child, a happy dog's wagging tail, or a warm, homecooked meal after a long day at school or work. Those living in the city may also find themselves distanced from the delights of nature—the sun, trees, leaves, flowers, fruits, insects, rivers, hills and valleys. They unfortunately lose out on the healing of a lush, green landscape, the soft tinkling of a water stream, the gleam of a starry, moonlit sky or a cosy bazaar during night time.

This book is about love, companionship, family, emotions, the magic of nature and the diverse shades of life. It will take you on an adventurous reading journey, letting you taste assorted flavours—joys, successes, failures, disappointments and heartbreaks. From personal anecdotes, to a sub inspector's thrilling story of betrayal, to a heartening story of friendship between two children belonging to entirely different worlds, this book presents to you, a delicious slice of life in all of its charms and imperfections!

Ruskin Bond

ADVENTURES IN READING

1

You don't see them so often now, those tiny books and almanacs—genuine pocket books—once so popular with our parents and grandparents; much smaller than the average paperback, often smaller than the palm of the hand. With the advent of coffee-table books, new books keep growing bigger and bigger, rivalling tombstones! And one day, like Alice after drinking from the wrong bottle, they will reach the ceiling and won't have anywhere else to go. The average publisher, who apparently believes that large profits are linked to large books, must look upon these old miniatures with amusement or scorn. They were not meant for a coffee table, true. They were meant for true book lovers and readers, for they took up very little space—you could slip them into your pocket without any discomfort, either to you or to the pocket.

I have a small collection of these little books, treasured over the years. Foremost is my father's prayer book and psalter, with his name, 'Aubrey Bond, Lovedale, 1917', inscribed on the inside back cover. Lovedale is a school in the Nilgiri Hills in South India, where, as a young man, he did his teacher's training. He gave it to me soon after I went to a boarding school in Shimla in 1944, and my own name is inscribed on it in his beautiful handwriting.

Another beautiful little prayer book in my collection is called *The Finger Prayer Book*. Bound in soft leather, it is about the same length and breadth as the average middle finger. Replete with psalms, it is the complete book of common prayer and not an abridgement; a marvel of miniature book production.

Not much larger is a delicate item in calf leather, *The Humour of Charles Lamb*. It fits into my wallet and often stays there. It has a tiny portrait of the great essayist, followed by some thirty to forty extracts from his essays, such as this favourite of mine: 'Every dead man must take upon himself to be lecturing me with his odious truism, that "Such as he is now, I must shortly be". Not so shortly, friend, perhaps as thou imaginest. In the meantime, I am alive. I move about. I am worth twenty of thee. Know thy betters!'

No fatalist, Lamb. He made no compromise with Father Time. He affirmed that in age, we must be as glowing and tempestuous as in youth! And yet Lamb is thought to be an old-fashioned writer.

Another favourite among my 'little' books is *The Pocket Trivet: An Anthology for Optimists*, published by *The Morning Post* newspaper in 1932. But what is a trivet? the unenlightened may well ask. Well, it's a stand for a small pot or kettle, fixed securely over a grate. To be right as a trivet is to be perfectly right. Just right, like the short sayings in this book, which are further enlivened by a number of charming woodcuts based on the seventeenth century originals, such as the illustration of a moth hovering over a candle flame and below it the legend—'I seeke mine owne hurt.'

But the sayings are mostly of a cheering nature, such as

Emerson's 'Hitch your wagon to a star' or the West Indian proverb: 'Every day no Christmas, an' every day no rainy day.'

My book of trivets is a happy example of much concentrated wisdom being collected in a small space—the beauty separated from the dross. It helps me to forget the dilapidated building in which I live and to look instead at the ever-changing cloud patterns as seen from my bedroom windows. There is no end to the shapes made by the clouds, or to the stories they set off in my head. We don't have to circle the world in order to find beauty and fulfilment. After all, most of living has to happen in the mind. And, to quote one anonymous sage from my trivet, 'The world is only the size of each man's head.'

2

Amongst the current fraternity of writers, I must be that very rare person—an author who actually writes by hand!

Soon after the invention of the typewriter, most editors and publishers understandably refused to look at any mansucript that was handwritten. A decade or two earlier, when Dickens and Balzac had submitted their hefty manuscrips in longhand, no one had raised any objection. Had their handwriting been awful, their manuscripts would still have been read. Fortunately for all concerned, most writers, famous or obscure, took pains over their handwriting. For some, it was an art in itself, and many of those early manuscripts are a pleasure to look at and read.

And it wasn't only authors who wrote with an elegant hand. Parents and grandparents of most of us had distinctive styles of their own. I still have my father's last letter, written to me when I was at boarding school in Shimla some fifty years ago. He used large, beautifully formed letters, and his thoughts seemed to have the same flow and clarity as his handwriting.

In his letter he advises me (then a nine-year-old) about my own handwriting: 'I wanted to write before about your writing. Ruskin... Sometimes I get letters from you in very small writing, as if you wanted to squeeze everything into one sheet of letter paper. It is not good for you or for your eyes, to get into the habit of writing too small... Try and form a larger style of handwriting—use more paper if necessary!'

I did my best to follow his advice, and I'm glad to report that after nearly forty years of the writing life, most people can still read my handwriting!

Word processors are all the rage now, and I have no objection to these mechanical aids any more than I have to my old Olympia typewriter, made in 1956 and still going strong. Although I do all my writing in longhand, I follow the conventions by typing a second draft. But I would not enjoy my writing if I had to do it straight on to a machine. It isn't just the pleasure of writing longhand. I like taking my notebooks and writing pads to odd places. This particular essay is being written on the steps of my small cottage facing Pari Tibba (Fairy Hill). Part of the reason for sitting here is that there is a new postman on this route, and I don't want him to miss me.

For a freelance writer, the postman is almost as important as a publisher. I could, of course, sit here doing nothing, but as I have pencil and paper with me, and feel like using them, I shall write until the postman comes and maybe after he has gone, too! There is really no way in which I could set up a word processor on these steps.

There are a number of favourite places where I do my writing. One is under the chestnut tree on the slope above the cottage. Word processors were not designed keeping mountain slopes in mind. But armed with a pen (or pencil) and paper, I can lie on the grass and write for hours. On one occasion last month, I did take my typewriter into the garden, and I am still trying to extricate an acorn from under the keys, while the roller seems permanently stained yellow with some fine pollen dust from the deodar trees.

My friends keep telling me about all the wonderful things I can do with a word processor, but they haven't got around to finding me one that I can take to bed, for that is another place where I do much of my writing—especially on cold winter nights, when it is impossible to keep the cottage warm.

While the wind howls outside, and snow piles up on the windowsill, I am warm under my quilt, writing pad on my knees, ballpoint pen at the ready. And if, next day, the weather is warm and sunny, these simple aids will accompany me on a long walk, ready for instant use should I wish to record an incident, a prospect, a conversation, or simply a train of thought.

When I think of the great eighteenth- and nineteenth-century writers, scratching away with their quill pens, filling hundreds of pages every month, I am amazed to find that their handwriting did not deteriorate into the sort of hieroglyphics that often make up the average doctor's prescription today. They knew they had to write legibly, if only for the sake of the typesetters.

Both Dickens and Thackeray had good, clear, flourishing styles. (Thackeray was a clever illustrator, too.) Somerset Maugham had an upright, legible hand. Churchill's neat handwriting never wavered, even when he was under stress. I like the bold, clear, straightforward hand of Abraham Lincoln; it mirrors the man. Mahatma Gandhi, another great soul who fell to the assassin's bullet, had many similarities of both handwriting and outlook.

Not everyone had a beautiful hand. King Henry VIII had an untidy scrawl, but then, he was not a man of much refinement. Guy Fawkes, who tried to blow up the British Parliament, had a very shaky hand. With such a quiver, no wonder he failed in his attempt! Hitler's signature is ugly, as you would expect. And Napoleon's doesn't seem to know where to stop; how much like the man!

I think my father was right when he said handwriting was often the key to a man's character, and that large, well-formed letters went with an uncluttered mind. Florence Nightingale had a lovely handwriting, the hand of a caring person. And there were many like her amongst our forebears.

3

When I was a small boy, no Christmas was really complete unless my Christmas stocking contained several recent issues of my favourite comic paper. If today my friends complain that I am too voracious a reader of books, they have only these comics to blame, for they were the origin, if not of my tastes in reading, then certainly of the reading habit itself.

I like to think that my conversion to comics began at the age of five, with a comic strip on the children's page of *The Statesman*. In the late 1930s, Benji, whose head later appeared only on the Benji League badge, had a strip to himself; I don't remember his adventures very clearly, but every day (or was it once a week?), I would cut out the Benji strip and paste it into a scrapbook. Two years later, this scrapbook, bursting with the adventures of Benji, accompanied me to boarding school, where, of course, it passed through several hands before finally passing into limbo.

Of course, comics did not form the only reading matter that found its way into my Christmas stocking. Before I was eight, I had read *Peter Pan, Alice's Adventures in Wonderland,* and most of *Mr Midshipman Easy*; but I had also consumed thousands of comic papers which were, after all, slim affairs and mostly pictorial, 'certain little penny books radiant with gold and rich with bad pictures', as Leigh Hunt described the children's papers of his own time.

But though they were mostly pictorial, comics in those days did have a fair amount of reading matter, too. *The Hotspur, The Wizard, The Magnet* (a victim of the Second World War) and *The Champion* contained stories woven round certain popular characters. In *The Champion*, which I read regularly right through my prep school years, there was Rockfist Rogan, Royal Air Force (R.A.F.), a pugilist who managed to combine boxing with bombing, and Fireworks Flynn, a footballer who always scored the winning goal in the last two minutes of play.

Billy Bunter has, of course, become one of the immortals— almost a subject for literary and social historians. Quite recently, *The Times Literary Supplement* devoted its first two pages to an analysis of the Bunter stories. Eminent lawyers and doctors still look back nostalgically to the arrival of the weekly *Magnet*; they are now the principal customers for the special souvenir edition of the first issue of the *Magnet*, recently reprinted in facsimile. Bunter, 'forever young', has become a folk hero. He is seen on stage, screen and television, and is even quoted in the House of Commons.

From this, I take courage. My only regret is that I did not preserve my own early comics—not because of any bibliophilic value which they might possess today, but because of my sentimental regard for early influences in art and literature.

The first venture in children's publishing, in 1774, was a comic of sorts. In that year, John Newberry brought out:

According to Act of Parliament (neatly bound and gilt): *A Little Pretty Pocket-Book, intended for the Amusement of Little Master Tommy and Pretty Miss Polly with Two Letters from Jack the Giant Killer.*

The book contained pictures, rhymes and games. Newberry's characters and imaginary authors included Woglog the Great Giant, Tommy Trip, Giles Gingerbread, Nurse Truelove, Peregrine Puzzlebrains, Primrose Prettyface, and many others with names similar to those found in the comic papers of our own century.

Newberry was also the originator of the 'Amazing Free Offer', so much a part of American comics. At the beginning of 1755, he had this to offer:

Nurse Truelove's New Year Gift, or the Book of Books for Children, adorned with Cuts and designed as a Present for every little boy who would become a great Man and ride upon a fine Horse; and to every little Girl who would become a great Woman and ride in a Lord Mayor's gilt Coach. Printed for the Author, who has ordered these books to be given gratis to all little Boys in St. Paul's churchyard, they paying for the Binding, which is only Two pence each Book.

Many of today's comics are crude and, like many television serials, violent in their appeal. But I did not know American comics until I was twelve, and by then, I had become quite discriminating. Superman, Bulletman, Batman and Green Lantern, and other super heroes all left me cold. I had, by then, passed into the world of real books but the weakness for the comic strip remains. I no longer receive comics in my Christmas stocking, but I do place a few in the stockings of Gautam and Siddharth. And, needless to say, I read them right through beforehand.

JOYFULLY I WRITE

I am a fortunate person. For over fifty years I have been able to make a living by doing what I enjoy most—writing.

Sometimes I wonder if I have written too much. One gets into the habit of serving up the same ideas over and over again, with a different sauce perhaps, but still the same ideas, themes, memories, characters. Writers are often chided for repeating themselves. Artists and musicians are given more latitude. No one criticized Turner for painting so many sunsets at sea, or Gauguin for giving us all those lovely Tahitian women, or Husain for treating us to so many horses, or Jamini Roy for giving us so many identical stylized figures.

In the world of music, one Puccini opera is very like another, a Chopin nocturne will return to familiar themes, and in the realm of lighter, modern music the same melodies recur with only slight variations. But authors are often taken to task for repeating themselves. They cannot help this, for in their writing they are expressing their personalities. Hemingway's world is very different from Jane Austen's. They are both unique worlds, but they do not change or mutate in the minds of their author-creators. Jane Austen spent all her life in one small place, and portrayed the people she knew. Hemingway roamed the world, but his characters remained much the same, usually extensions of himself.

In the course of a long writing career, it is inevitable that a writer will occasionally repeat himself, or return to themes that have remained with him even as new ideas and formulations enter his mind. The important thing is to keep writing, observing, listening and paying attention to the beauty of words and their arrangement. And, like artists and musicians, the more we work on our art, the better it will be.

Writing, for me, is the simplest and greatest pleasure in the world. Putting a mood or an idea into words is an occupation I truly love. I plan my day so that there is time in it for writing a poem, or a paragraph, or an essay, or part of a story or longer work; not just because writing is my profession, but from a feeling of delight.

The world around me—be it the mountains or the busy street below my window—is teeming with subjects, sights, thoughts, that I wish to put into words in order to catch the fleeting moment, the passing image, the laughter, the joy, and sometimes, the sorrow. Life would be intolerable if I did not have this freedom to write every day. Not that everything I put down is worth preserving. A great many pages of manuscripts have found their way into my waste-paper basket or into the stove that warms the family room on cold winter evenings. I do not always please myself. I cannot always please others because, unlike the hard professionals, the Forsyths and the Sheldons, I am not writing to please everyone, I am really writing to please myself!

My theory of writing is that the conception should be as clear as possible, and that words should flow like a stream of clear water, preferably a mountain stream! You will, of course, encounter boulders, but you will learn to go over them or around them, so that your flow is unimpeded. If your stream gets too sluggish or muddy, it is better to put aside that particular piece of writing. Go to the source, go to the spring, where the water is purest, your thoughts as clear as the mountain air.

I do not write for more than an hour or two in the course of the day. Too long at the desk, and words lose their freshness.

Together with clarity and a good vocabulary, there must come a certain elevation of mood. Sterne must have been bubbling over with high spirits when he wrote *Tristram Shandy.* The sombre intensity of *Wuthering Heights* reflects Emily Brontë's passion for life, fully knowing that it was to be brief. Tagore's melancholy comes through in his poetry. Dickens is always passionate; there are no half measures in his work. Conrad's prose takes on the moods of the sea he knew and loved.

A real physical emotion accompanies the process of writing, and great writers are those who can channel this emotion into the creation of their best work.

'Are you a serious writer?' a schoolboy once asked.

'Well, I try to be *serious*,' I said, 'but cheerfulness keeps breaking in!'

Can a cheerful writer be taken seriously? I don't know. But I was certainly serious about making writing the main occupation of my life.

In order to do this, one has to give up many things—a job, security, comfort, domesticity—or rather, the pursuit of these things. Had I married when I was twenty-five, I would not have been able to throw up a good job as easily as I did at the time; I might now be living on a pension! God forbid. I am grateful for continued independence and the necessity to keep writing for my living, and for those who share their lives with me and whose joys and sorrows are mine too. An artist must not lose his hold on life. We do that when we settle for the safety of a comfortable old age.

Normally writers do not talk much, because they are saving their conversation for the readers of their books—those invisible listeners with whom we wish to strike a sympathetic chord. Of course, we talk freely with our friends, but we are reserved with people we do not know very well. If I talk too freely about a story I am going to write, chances are it will never be written. I have talked it to death.

Being alone is vital for any creative writer. I do not mean that you must live the life of a recluse. People who do not know me are frequently under the impression that I live in lonely splendour on a mountain top, whereas in reality, I share a small flat with a family of twelve—and I'm the twelfth man, occasionally bringing out refreshments for the players!

I love my extended family, every single individual in it, but as a writer, I must sometimes get a little time to be alone with my own thoughts, reflect a little, talk to myself, laugh about all the blunders I have committed in the past, and ponder over the future. This is contemplation, not meditation. I am not very good at meditation, as it involves remaining in a passive state for some time. I would rather be out walking, observing the natural world, or sitting under a tree contemplating my novel or navel! I suppose the latter is a form of meditation.

When I casually told a journalist that I planned to write a book consisting of my meditations, he reported that I was writing a book on meditation per se, which gave it a different connotation. I shall go along with the simple dictionary meaning of the verb *meditate*—to plan mentally, to exercise the mind in contemplation.

So I was doing it all along!

◆

I am not, by nature, a gregarious person. Although I love people, and have often made friends with complete strangers, I am also a lover of solitude. Naturally, one thinks better when one is alone. But I prefer walking alone to walking with others. That ladybird on the wild rose would escape my attention if I was engaged in a lively conversation with a companion. Not that the ladybird is going to change my life. But by acknowledging its presence, stopping to admire its beauty, I have paid obeisance to the natural scheme of things of which I am only a small part.

It is upon a person's power of holding fast to such undimmed beauty that his or her inner hopefulness depends. As we journey through the world, we must inevitably encounter meanness and selfishness. As we fight for our survival, the higher visions and ideals often fade. It is then that we need ladybirds! Contemplating that tiny creature, or the flower on which it rests, gives one the hope—better, the certainty—that there is more to life than interest rates, dividends, market forces and infinite technology.

As a writer, I have known hope and despair, success and failure; some recognition, but also long periods of neglect and critical dismissal. But I have had no regrets. I have enjoyed the writer's life to the full, and one reason for this is that living in India has given me certain freedoms which I would not have enjoyed elsewhere. Friendship when needed. Solitude when desired. Even, at times, love and passion. It has tolerated me for what I am—a bit of a dropout, unconventional, idiosyncratic. I have been left alone to do my own thing. In India, people do not censure you unless you start making a nuisance of yourself. Society has its norms and its orthodoxies, and provided you do not flaunt all the rules, society will allow you to go your own way. I am free to become a naked ascetic and roam the streets with a begging bowl; I am also free to live in a palatial farmhouse if I have the wherewithal. For twenty-five years, I have lived in this small, sunny second-floor room looking out on the mountains, and no one has bothered me, unless you count the neighbour's dog who prevents the postman and courier boys from coming up the steps.

◆

I may write for myself, but as I also write to get published, it must follow that I write for others too. Only a handful of readers might enjoy my writing, but they are my soulmates, my alter egos, and they keep me going through those lean times and discouraging moments.

Even though I depend upon my writing for a livelihood, it is still, for me, the most delightful thing in the world.

I did not set out to make a fortune from writing; I knew I was not that kind of writer. But it was the thing I did best, and I persevered with the exercise of my gift, cultivating the more discriminating editors, publishers and readers, never really expecting huge rewards but accepting whatever came my way. Happiness is a matter of temperament rather than circumstance, and I have always considered myself fortunate in having escaped the tedium of a nine-to-five job or some other form of drudgery.

Of course, there comes a time when almost every author asks himself what his effort and output really amounts to. We expect our work to influence people, to affect a great many readers, when in fact, its impact is infinitesimal. Those who work on a large scale must feel discouraged by the world's indifference. That is why I am happy to give a little innocent pleasure to a handful of readers. This is a reward worth having.

As a writer, I have difficulty in doing justice to momentous events, the wars of nations, the politics of power; I am more at ease with the dew of the morning, the sensuous delights of the day, the silent blessings of the night, the joys and sorrows of children, the strivings of ordinary folk and, of course, the ridiculous situations in which we sometimes find ourselves.

We cannot prevent sorrow and pain and tragedy. And yet when we look around us, we find that the majority of people are actually enjoying life! There are so many lovely things to see, there is so much to do, so much fun to be had, and so many charming and interesting people to meet... How can my pen ever run dry?

A BOOK LOVER'S LIFELONG HUNT

My mother and stepfather were not great readers, and books were a scarce commodity in my life until I was about twelve. In those lonely childhood years, I was to discover that books could be good friends, steadfast and reliable, and I seized upon almost any printed matter that came my way, whether it was a girls' classic like *Little Women*, or a *True Detective* magazine, or Edgar Allan Poe, or 'Insect Life in Mozambique'.

Fifty years on, my reading habits are still as wide-ranging and omnivorous.

But I think it all began in that forest rest house in the Siwalik Hills, a subtropical range cradling the Doon Valley in northern India. Here, my stepfather and his gun-toting friends were given to hunting the wild animals that still roamed those forests. He was a poor shot, so he cannot really be blamed for the absence of wildlife today; but he did his best to shoot down everything in sight!

On one of these 'shikar' trips, we were staying in a rest house near the Timli Pass. My stepfather and his friends were 'after the tiger', and set out every morning with an army of villagers to 'beat' the jungle, in order to drive the tiger out into the open. Never excited by this form of sport, I stayed behind in the rest house, fully expecting complete boredom for the duration of our stay. Exploring the old rest house, I discovered that one of the rooms was furnished with a dusty bookshelf, stacked high with books that hadn't been touched for years.

It was here that I discovered *Three Men in a Boat*, by Jerome K. Jerome, which I finished reading that same day. The next day, I read most of the stories in M.R. James' *Ghost Stories of an Antiquary*. On the third day, while the sportsmen were still looking for their tiger, I chuckled over my first Wodehouse (*Love Among the Chickens*), sampled O. Henry, and began *David Copperfield*. Camp broke up before I could get through *Copperfield*, but the forest ranger said I could keep it, which I did, thus becoming the only person with a trophy to show for the hunt, the clever tiger having proved elusive.

After that adventure, I was always looking for books in unlikely places; and I had a knack of finding them, too.

A couple of years ago, I was rummaging through some discarded books at a school jumble sale, when I found a first edition of *Three Men in a Boat*. As this book had been one of my first loves, I felt that my reading adventures had come full cycle. When I think of all the great books I have read over the years, I realize that they have more than made up for the disappointments that sometimes came my way, and that I am indeed a fortunate man. I am sure that other compulsive readers feel the same way.

Although I never went to college, I think I have read as much, if not more, than most college men, so that it would be true to say that I received my education in second-hand bookshops. London had many, and Calcutta once had a number of them, but I think the prize must go to a small town in Wales called Hay-on-Wye, which has twenty-six bookshops and over one million books. It's in the world's quieter corners that book lovers still flourish as a race.

Unlikely, out-of-the-way places often yield up treasures—like the trunkful thrown out of a hotel storeroom, providing me with *The Complete Plays of J.M. Barrie*. Am I the only person around who still reads Barrie? His occasional sentimentality is a sin in the eyes of modern critics, but I must confess to an unabashed enjoyment of plays such as *Mary Rose*, *Dear Brutus*, *A Kiss For Cinderella*, and, of course, *Peter Pan*.

I love discovering forgotten or neglected gems, which I feel deserve to be read again. One of them was an exquisite essay by the Boston writer, Louise Imogen Guiney (1861–1920), called 'The Precept of Peace', which appeared in her book *Patrins* (1897). A lovely and profound piece of writing, it is typical of the humorous tranquillity with which she faced the failure (financially speaking) of all her books.

Another gem, *Sweet Rocket* (1920) by Mary Johnston, was also a financial failure. It had only the thinnest outline of a story, but she set out her ideas in lyrical prose that seduces the sympathetic reader at every turn of the page. Miss Johnston was from Virginia. She did not travel outside America. But her little book did. I found it buried under a pile of railway timetables at a railway bookstall in Simla, the old summer capital of India—almost as though it had been waiting there for me, these seventy years!

LOVE THY CRITIC

Having just read a nasty review of my last book in *India Today*, I take heart by recalling Hemingway's direct action against critic Max Eastman in 1937. Eastman had questioned Hemingway's manhood in his review of *Death in the Afternoon*, which he had sarcastically titled 'Bull in the Afternoon'.

When Hemingway saw Eastman, he bashed him over the head with a copy of the book and then wrestled him to the ground. Trouble is, my critic is a woman. I'd lose the wrestling match.

This sort of response is rare, but exchanges between authors and critics can get nasty, with reputations maligned and genuine talents belittled. The worst sort of reviewers are those who make personal attacks on authors, usually a sign of envy coupled with malice. Thomas Carlyle called Emerson 'a hoary-headed and toothless baboon' and wrote of Charles Lamb: 'a more pitiful, rickety, gasping, staggering Tomfool I do not know.' But we still read and enjoy Lamb and Emerson; who reads Carlyle?

Of Walt Whitman, one reviewer said: 'Whitman is as unacquainted with art as a hog is with mathematics.' Swift was accused of having 'a diseased mind' and Henry James was called an 'idiot and a Boston idiot to boot, than which there is nothing lower in the world'. Their critics have long been forgotten, but just occasionally an author turns critic with equal virulence. There was the classic Dorothy Parker review which read: 'This is not a novel to be tossed aside lightly. It should be thrown with great force.'

When brickbats are flung at an author, it is usually a sign that he or she is successful, has reached the top. No one received more abuse than Shakespeare. *Hamlet* was described by Voltaire as 'the work of a drunken savage', and Pepys said *A Midsummer Night's Dream* was 'the most insipid, ridiculous play that I ever saw in my life'. Macaulay sneered at Wordsworth's 'crazy mystical metaphysics, the endless wilderness of dull, flat, prosaic twaddle', a description that would aptly describe Macaulay's own meandering and monotonous style.

Should authors really have to put up with this sort of thing? Politicians do, and actors and sportsmen, so why not writers? As E.M. Forster once said: 'No author has the right to whine. He was not obliged to be an author. He invited publicity, and he must take the publicity that comes along.'

Of course, some reviewers do go a little too far, like the one who once referred to 'that well-known typist Harold Robbins'.

That was a remark truly deserving a bash over the head, on behalf of typists everywhere.

Writing for a living: it's a battlefield!

People do ask funny questions. Accosted on the road by a stranger, who proceeds to cross-examine me, starting with: 'Excuse me, are you a good writer?' For once, I'm stumped for an answer.

A GOOD PHILOSOPHY

The other day, when I was with a group of students, a bright young thing asked me, 'Sir, what is your philosophy of life?' She had me stumped.

There I was, a seventy-five-year-old, still writing, and still functioning physically and mentally (or so I believed), but quite helpless when it came to formulating 'a philosophy of life'.

How dare I reach the venerable age of seventy-five without a philosophy; without anything resembling a religious outlook; without arming myself with a battery of great thoughts to impress my young interlocutor, who is obviously in need of a little practical if not spiritual guidance to help her navigate the shoals of life.

This morning, I was pondering on this absence of a philosophy or religious outlook in my make-up, and feeling a little low because it was cloudy and dark outside, and gloomy weather always seems to dampen my spirits. Then the clouds broke up and the sun came out—large, yellow splashes of sunshine in my room and upon my desk, and almost immediately I felt an uplift of spirit. And at the same time I realized that no philosophy would be of any use to a person so susceptible to changes in light and shade, sunshine and shadow. I was a pagan, pure and simple; a sensualist; sensitive to touch and colour and fragrance and odour and sounds of every description; a creature of instinct, of spontaneous attractions, given to illogical fancies and attachments. As a guide, philosopher and friend, I am of no use to anyone, least of all to myself.

I think the best advice I ever had was contained in these lines from Shakespeare, which my father had copied into one of my notebooks when I was nine years old:

'This above all: to thine own self be true,
And it must follow, as the night of the day,
Thou canst not then be false to any man.'

Each one of us is a mass of imperfections, and to be able to recognize and live with our imperfections, our basic natures, defects of genes and birth—hereditary flaws—makes for an easier transit on life's journey.

I am always a little wary of saints and godmen, preachers and teachers, who are ready with solutions for all our problems. For one thing, they talk too much. When I was at school, I mastered the art of sleeping (without appearing to sleep) through a long speech or lecture by the principal or visiting dignitary, and I must confess to doing the same thing today. The trick is to sleep with your eyes half closed; this gives the impression of concentrating very hard on what is being said, even though you might well be roaming happily in dreamland.

In our imperfect world, there is far too much talk and not enough thought.

The TV channels are awash with TV gurus telling us how to live, and they do so at great length. This verbal diarrhoea is infectious and appears to affect newspersons and TV anchors who are prone to lecturing and bullying the guests on their shows. Too many know-alls. A philosophy for living? You won't find it on your TV sets. You will learn more from a cab driver or street vendor.

'And what's your philosophy?' I asked my sabziwalla, as he weighed out a kilo of onions.

'Philosophy? What's that?' He turned to his assistant. 'Is this gentleman trying to abuse me?'

'No, sir,' I said. 'It's not a term of abuse. I was just asking— are you a happy man?'

'Why do you want to know? Are you from the income tax department?'

'No, I'm just a storyteller. So tell me—what makes you happy?'

'A good customer,' he said. 'So tell me—what makes *you* happy?'

'The same thing, I suppose,' I had to confess. 'A good publisher!' I did not tell him about the sunshine, the birdsong, the bedside book, the potted geranium, and all the other little things that make life worth living. It's better that he finds out for himself.

RUNNING FOR COVER

The right to privacy is a fine concept and might actually work in the West, but in Eastern lands it is purely notional. If I want to be left alone, I have to be a shameless liar, pretend that I am out of town or, if that doesn't work, announce that I have measles, mumps or some new variety of Asian flu.

Now I happen to like people and I like meeting people from all walks of life. If this were not the case, I would have nothing to write about. But I don't like too many people all at once. They tend to get in the way. And if they arrive without warning, banging on my door while I am in the middle of composing a poem or writing a story, or simply enjoying my afternoon siesta, I am inclined to be snappy or unwelcoming. Occasionally, I have even turned people away.

As I get older, that afternoon siesta becomes more of a necessity and less of an indulgence. But it's strange how people love to call on me between two and four in the afternoon. I suppose it's the time of day when they have nothing to do.

'How do we get through the afternoon?' one of them will say.

'I know! Let's go and see old Ruskin. He's sure to entertain us with some stimulating conversation, if nothing else.' Stimulating conversation in mid-afternoon? Even Socrates would have balked at it.

'I'm sorry I can't see you today,' I mutter. 'I don't feel at all well.' (In fact, extremely unwell at the prospect of several strangers gaping at me for at least half-an-hour.)

'Not well? We're so sorry. My wife here is a homeopath.'

It's amazing, the number of homeopaths who turn up at my door. Unfortunately, they never seem to have their little powders on them, those miracle cures for everything, from headaches to hernias.

The other day, a family burst in—uninvited of course. The husband was an ayurvedic physician, the wife was a homeopath (naturally), the eldest boy, a medical student at an allopathic medical college.

'What do you do when one of you falls ill?' I asked, 'Do you try all three systems of medicine?'

'It depends on the ailment,' said the young man. 'But we seldom fall ill. My sister here is a yoga expert.'

His sister, a hefty girl in her late twenties (still single) looked more like an all-in wrestler than a supple yoga practitioner. She looked at my tummy. She could see I was in bad shape.

'I could teach you some exercises,' she said. 'But you'd have to come to Ludhiana.'

I felt grateful that Ludhiana was a six-hour drive from Mussoorie.

'I'll drop in some day,' I said. 'In fact, I'll come and take a course.'

We parted on excellent terms. But it doesn't always turn out that way.

There was this woman, very persistent, in fact downright rude, who wouldn't go away even when I told her I had bird-flu.

'I have to see you,' she said, 'I've written a novel, and I want you to recommend it for a Booker Prize.'

'I'm afraid I have no influence there,' I pleaded. 'I'm completely unknown in Britain.'

'Then how about the Nobel Prize?'

I thought about that for a minute. 'Only in the science field,' I said. 'If it's something to do with genes or stem cells?'

She looked at me as though I was some kind of worm. 'You are not very helpful,' she said.

'Well, let me read your book.'

'I haven't written it yet.'

'Well, why not come back when it's finished? Give yourself a year—two years—these things should never be done in a hurry.' I guided her to the gate and encouraged her down the steps.

'You are very rude,' she said. 'You did not even ask me in. I'll report you to Khushwant Singh. He's a friend of mine. He'll put you in his column.'

'If Khushwant Singh is your friend,' I said, 'why are you bothering with me? He knows all the Nobel and Booker Prize people. All the important people, in fact.'

I did not see her again, but she got my phone number from someone, and now she rings me once a week to tell me her book is coming along fine. Any day now, she's going to turn up with the manuscript.

Casual visitors who bring me their books or manuscripts are the ones I dread most. They ask me for an opinion, and if I give them a frank assessment, they resent it. It's unwise to tell a would-be writer that his memoirs or novel or collected verse would be better off unpublished. Murders have been committed for less. So I play safe and say, 'Very promising. Carry on writing.' But this is fatal. Almost immediately, I am asked to write a foreword or introduction, together with a letter of recommendation to my publisher—or any publisher of standing. Unwillingly, I become a literacy agent; unpaid, of course.

I am all for encouraging the arts and literature, but I do think writers should seek out their own publishers and write their own introductions.

The perils of doing this sort of thing were illustrated when 1 was prevailed upon to write a short introduction to a book about a dreaded man-eater who had taken a liking to the flesh of the good people of Dogadda, near Lansdowne. The author of the book could hardly write a decent sentence, but he managed to string together a lengthy account of the leopard's depradations. He was so persistent, calling on me or ringing me up, that I finally did the introduction. He then wanted me to edit or touch up his manuscript; but this I refused to do. I would starve if I had to sit down and rewrite other people's books. But he prevailed upon me to give him a photograph.

Months later, the book appeared, printed privately of course. And there was my photograph, and a photograph of the dead leopard after it had been hunted down. But the local printer had got the captions mixed up. The dead animal's picture earned the line: 'Well-known author Ruskin Bond.' My picture carried the legend: 'Dreaded man-eater, shot after it had killed its 26th victim.'

The printer's devil had turned me into a serial killer.

Now you know why I'm wary of writing introductions.

'Vanity' publishers thrive on writers who are desperate to see their work in print. They will print and deliver a book at your doorstep and then leave you with the task of selling it; or to be more accurate, disposing of it.

One of my neighbours, Mrs Santra—may her soul rest in peace—paid a publisher forty-thousand rupees to bring out a fancy edition of her late husband's memoirs. During his lifetime, he'd been unable to get it published, but before he died, he got his wife to promise that she'd publish it for him. This she did, and the publisher duly delivered 500 copies to the good lady. She gave a few copies to friends, and then passed away, leaving the books behind. Her heir is now saddled with 450 hardbound volumes of unsaleable memoirs.

I have always believed that if a writer is any good he will find a publisher who will print, bind and sell his books, and even give him a royalty for his efforts. A writer who pays to get published is inviting disappointment and heartbreak.

Many people are under the impression that I live in splendour in a large mansion, surrounded by secretaries and servants. They are disappointed to find that I live in a tiny bedroom-cum-study and that my living room is so full of books that there is hardly space for more than three or four visitors at a time.

Sometimes, thirty to forty schoolchildren turn up, wanting to see me. I don't turn away children, if I can help it. But if they come in large numbers, I have to meet and talk to them on the road, which is inconvenient for everyone.

If I had the means, would I live in a splendid mansion in the more affluent parts of Mussoorie, with a film star or TV personality as my neighbour? I rather doubt it. All my life I've been living in one or two rooms and I don't think I could manage a bigger establishment. True, my extended family takes up another two rooms, but they see to it that my working space is not violated. And if I am hard at work (or fast asleep), they will try to protect me from unheralded or unwelcome visitors.

And I have learnt to tell lies. Especially when I'm asked to attend school functions as a chief guest or in some formal capacity. To spend two or three hours listening to speeches (and then being expected to give one) is my idea of hell. It's hell for the students and it's hell for me. The speeches are usually followed (or preceded) by folk dances, musical interludes or class plays, and this only adds to the torment. Sports days are just as bad. You can skip the speeches (hopefully), but you must sit out in the hot sun for the greater part of the day, while a loudspeaker informs you that little Parshottam has just broken the school record for the under-nine high jump, or that Pamela Highjinks has won the hurdles for the third year running. You don't get to see the events because you are kept busy making polite conversation with the other guests. The only occasion when a sports' event really came to life was when a misdirected discus narrowly missed decapitating the headmaster's wife.

Former athletes and sportsmen seldom visit me. They have difficulty making it up my steps. Most of them have problems with their knees before they are fifty. They hobble (for want of a better word). Once their playing days are over, they start hobbling. Nandu, a former tennis champion, can't make it up my steps, nor can Chand, a former wrestler. Too much physical activity when young, has resulted in an early breakdown of the body's machinery. As Nandu says, 'Body can't take it any more.' I'm not too agile either, but then, I was never much of a sportsman. Second last in the marathon was probably my most memorable achievement.

Oddly enough, some of the most frequent visitors to my humble abode are honeymooners.

Why, I don't know, but they always ask for my blessing even though I am hardly an advertisement for married bliss. A seventy-year-old bachelor blessing a newly married couple? Maybe they are under the impression that I'm a Brahmachari?

But how would that help them? They are going to have babies sooner or later.

It is seldom that they happen to be readers or book-lovers, so why pick an author, and that too, one who does not go to places of worship? However, since these young couples are inevitably attractive, and full of high hopes for their future and the future of mankind, I am happy to talk to them, wish them well...and if it's a blessing they want, they are welcome. My hands are far from being saintly, but at least they are well-intentioned.

I have, at times, been mistaken for other people.

'Are you Mr Pickwick?' asked a small boy. At least he'd been reading Dickens. A distant relative, I said, and beamed at him in my best Pickwickian manner.

I am at ease with children, who talk quite freely except when accompanied by their parents. Then it's mum and dad who do all the talking.

'My son studies your book in school,' said one fond mother, proudly exhibiting her ten-year-old. 'He wants your autograph.'

'What's the name of the book you're reading?' I asked.

'Tom Sawyer,' he said promptly.

So I signed Mark Twain in his autograph book. He seemed quite happy.

A schoolgirl asked me to autograph her maths textbook.

'But I failed in maths,' I said. 'I'm just a story writer.'

'How much did you get?'

'Four out of a hundred.'

She looked at me rather crossly and snatched the book away.

I have signed books in the names of Enid Blyton, R.K. Narayan, Ian Botham, Daniel Defoe, Harry Potter and the Swiss Family Robinson. No one seems to mind.

THE OLD SUITCASE

The autobiography of my suitcase is, in many respects, my own autobiography.

I bought it in Jersey, in the Channel Islands, in 1952, and for well over sixty-five years it has given shelter to so many of my personal effects—socks, underwear, shirts, trousers; books, notebooks, pens, paper, passport; and in recent years (when, like its owner, it is showing signs of wear and tear), a receptacle for old manuscripts, photographs, newspaper cuttings, publishers' contracts, and the flotsam of a lifetime of putting pen to paper.

For the last few years, the suitcase had lain under my bed, so forgotten that the mice had managed to get in, building a nest from old newspapers; and I was woken one night by the squealing of baby mice—several of them. I was about to evict the family when I remembered the times when I had been evicted from lodgings, so I allowed them a respite of several days—a sort of stay order—before tipping the lot into an empty flowerpot and hoping for the best.

The suitcase was in a sad condition, but I was loath to throw it away. You don't throw away old friends. Or do you? There are all-weather friends and there are fair-weather friends, and it can take time to tell one from the other. The old suitcase had been with one long enough to be called both friend and philosopher, and so I hung on to it.

◆

It was a very cheap suitcase—the cheapest I could find in that Woolworth's Store in Jersey, when I was eighteen and ready to try my luck in London. I had spent a year in Jersey, living with my aunt's family and working as a junior clerk in the Public Health Department. Late evening, I'd sit down at my small portable typewriter (bought with the help of a loan from Mr Bromley, a kind senior clerk) and work on the novel that I was writing—the novel that was to become *The Room on the Roof;* but I was keen to move to London, where there were publishers and writers and bookshops and theatres, and I was saving something out of my weekly wage of £3 in order to make that dream a reality.

I had saved about £12 when a decision to leave was forced upon me as result of a quarrel I had with my uncle, a good man but somewhat set in his way of thinking.

I used to keep a diary at the time, and I'd made the mistake of leaving it on my desk near the typewriter in the attic room where I worked. My uncle, prowling around while I was out at work, had come across and read some entries in which I had expressed dissatisfaction with his narrow-mindedness and extreme political views. He confronted me with the diary. He accused me of being an ingrate and a 'nigger lover' (his words) and suggested that I leave his house.

So, of course, I took up his suggestion, gave a week's notice to the Public Health Department, and packed my belongings. Jersey was not for me.

But I needed a suitcase—and a cheap one. The tin trunk

I had brought from India was unsuitable for travelling about in England, where you had to manage your own luggage. The suitcase I found was very light—made of some sort of reinforced hardboard—and I did not expect it to last very long. But it was big enough for my few belongings, and it cost £2 and a few shillings.

And so, with my new suitcase in my right hand, and the typewriter in my left hand, I boarded the ferry for Southampton, and eight hours later, found myself on the train to London—without a job, without a home to go to, and with a half-written novel as my only asset.

◆

The gales of Jersey were exchanged for the fog of London. March is probably the most dismal month in that hardy city—fog outside, and indoors, the smell of leaking gas. Continuous drizzle. Aspidistras growing in dark corners of boarding-house entrance halls. The sun, a distant memory. I cursed myself for leaving India.

An old school friend put me up in his small room for almost a month. He loved cooking, and the room was always full of the fragrance of curries and spices. I found a job and a room of my own, and typewriter, suitcase, and I ascended the stairs to a tiny attic room in a boarding house in Glenmore Road.

It was a depressing little room, but I was out most of the day, working in an office in distant Soho, or wandering about looking for cheap cafés, living off beans on toast or 'meat and two veg'—the staple chow in the ABC restaurants. When I had money to spare I went to the cinema. Everyone smoked in those days, and it was difficult to see the screen through the haze of smoke that drifted through the hall.

I left Glenmore Road for Haverstock Hill, my suitcase getting heavier with the few books that I had been acquiring. At night, I worked on my novel—the first draft written by hand, the second draft typed out on my little portable.

Diana Athill, a partner in the firm of Andre Deutsch, and about fifteen years my senior, befriended me and had me over for dinner on several occasions. She gave me an old raincoat—we were about the same height—and out of gratitude, I showed her how to make a curry. I think it was more of a stew than a curry, but we managed to consume it.

Then the three friends—suitcase, typewriter, and budding author—moved to Tooting, in South London.

Why Tooting?

Well, I'd fallen in love with this wonderful girl from Vietnam. She was a student and her name was Vu-Phuong, meaning 'like the wind', and true enough, she came and went like the wind.

She was sweet company, and for several weeks, we spent a lot of time together—strolling in Kensington Gardens, wandering through the hothouses in Kew, even going to the opera. It was my suggestion that we go to the opera. The cheaper seats were right at the back of the huge opera house, and we couldn't hear much of the singing, not even the rollicking Toreador song (it was *Carmen*)—it was much better on gramophone records!

On a rainy day in June, we joined the crowds on the streets, watching Queen Elizabeth's coach pass by in all its splendour. Vu had a pretty umbrella and I had Diana Athill's raincoat, so we did not mind the rain.

And then, unaccountably, Vu stopped seeing me. She even changed her lodgings without giving me her new address. I tried to trace her, but without any success. Then I received a note from her saying she was returning to her home in Hanoi.

The Vietnam War was at its height, and Hanoi was part of Communist-held territory. It was possible that she was under pressure to avoid contact with 'Westerners'. I was no Westerner, but how were her political bosses to know that? Heartbroken, I left Tooting—how I hated Tooting!—and returned to the more familiar streets of Belsize Park.

I told Diana of my unhappy plight—I would often confide in her—and to cheer me up, she took me to St Paul's Cathedral to hear Yehudi Menuhin, the great violinist, give a recital. It was a moving experience, and for once I felt grateful to London for giving me the opportunity to hear great music.

◆

Another kind of music assailed me when I made friends with a bunch of West Indians, newly arrived in England. They invited me to a calypso party in a flat in Brixton (right next to the prison), and the dancing and revelry continued till dawn. Unthinking, I invited them to hold their next party in my bedsitter (now a fairly spacious one) in Belsize Park. The party was a great success, the building shuddered to its foundations as the rum flowed and the dancing grew frenetic, and the next day my landlord gave me twenty-four-hours' notice to leave the premises.

I lugged my suitcase and typewriter down the road to Swiss Cottage, where a kindly Jewish landlady (my third Jewish landlady) took me in and gave me a pleasant room with a large window which let in the sunlight on those few occasions when the sun came out. She even gave me a good breakfast. But she warned me against having parties in the room. And no lady visitors. And no pin-ups on the walls. Down came Eartha Kitt.

I was quite happy in Swiss Cottage, but after nearly four years away from India, I felt it was time to go home.

'No job for you here,' my mother had warned me. 'And you won't make any money from writing. Better stay in England.'

But I was not to be put off. Home is where the heart is, and my heart was still in the foothills of Dehra.

After much dithering, Diana and Andre Deutsch gave me a cheque for £50 as an advance against my novel, which had finally been accepted. This was the standard advance in those days. Publication was still a year off, but I did not feel like hanging around in London any longer. The fare to Bombay—by the cheapest passenger liner, the *M. S. Batory*, a Polish ship—was just under £40. I bought a ticket, gave a week's notice to my employer, thanked Diana for her many kindnesses, and bought a second suitcase.

This new suitcase cost more than the old one, and was quite flashy, but it was not to last as long. The cheap hardboard suitcase had accompanied me all over London, from one boarding house to another, and had attached itself to me like an unwanted stray, knowing no one else would keep it.

◆

The *M. S. Batory* had a reputation for being unlucky, and even before it sailed, half the crew had sought political asylum in the UK. But it had a good bar, serving Polish vodka, and only one passenger fell overboard in the course of the voyage.

At Gibraltar, I went ashore and bought several bottles of perfume from an Indian trader. These, I thought, would make suitable presents for friends and family. At Port Said, I went ashore and had my pocket picked; fortunately I'd kept most of my money in the old suitcase. At Aden, I went ashore and did nothing; there was nothing to do and nothing to see. At Bombay, I stepped ashore with my suitcases and was met by a couple of young customs officials and told to open them. I did so, and they took away all my bottles of perfume. Contraband, they said.

Happy homecoming!

'What will they do with it?' I asked a fellow passenger.

'Give it all to their girlfriends this evening,' he said knowingly.

At least they left my typewriter alone. And suitcases, typewriter, and I arrived in Dehradun without further mishap. I had no presents for anyone, but I was welcomed back anyway.

◆

And so began three years of freelancing, bombarding every magazine and newspaper in the land with stories, articles, and anything they would publish and pay for! The little typewriter broke down from all the strain, the letter 'b' breaking off; being irreplaceable, I had to go through all my typescripts and fill in the 'b's' by hand. Stories and articles would only be considered if typed, so I had no choice but to go through with this chore, cursing all the time, the letter 'b' being most appropriate for this purpose: 'Bugger the bloody B!' In all my years of writing, I have never used swear words in print—and now, here I am doing just that!

While my typewriter was getting a battering, the suitcase was enjoying a well-earned rest. It was put to use again when I moved to Delhi for three or four years, a period when my creative efforts were at their lowest ebb. As a writer I am greatly influenced by my surroundings and environment, and the Delhi (or rather, New Delhi) of the 1960s failed to get my creative juices flowing.

There was only one thing to do—pack up, and take to the hills.

It was a wise move although not always a restful one. Landlords, leaking roofs, crumbling hillsides and water shortages, all involved moving from one dwelling to another—Maplewood Lodge, Wayside Cottage (on the old Kipling Road), a flat near the Mall, then up to Landour's Prospect Point and down again to Ivy Cottage! The old suitcase was kept fairly busy, now used more as a receptacle for books and papers. The latches had rusted away and I had to use a length of rope to close the suitcase; but it held up wonderfully well, although it was just reinforced hardboard.

For several years, it was located under my bed, and whenever I came across some interesting relic, by way of an old magazine or newspaper, I would store it away for reference. My collection included *The Madras Mail* annual of 1926, an issue of *The Statesman* (1936, I think) reporting on the horrors of the Quetta earthquake, and a copy of *Life* (1947) carrying a feature on the changes that were taking place in India at the time of Independence. This had a picture of me, looking very angelic, saying my prayers in the school chapel of Bishop Cotton School, Simla, referred to in the article as the 'Eton of the East'. I think I was chosen for the picture partly because I looked angelic and partly because I was one of the handful of English-looking boys left in the school. But there was nothing angelic about me when I was thirteen, just as there is nothing angelic about me now.

Over a period of time, the mice had managed to gnaw their way through the fabric of the suitcase and had made a neat little home for themselves among my souvenirs. As they did no great damage, I left them alone, live and let live always having been my motto.

Then last month, we had a terrible storm. The window burst open, the glass fell out, the rain came pouring into the room, and by morning, the suitcase was half-full of water. The mice had already gone, but everything made of paper had been ruined and had to be thrown away.

The suitcase was put out to dry on the verandah, but it did not look as though it would recover.

'Shall I throw it away?' asked Beena, my granddaughter. 'It's falling to pieces.'

Do you throw away an old friend just because he's a cripple and of no use to anyone any more? For over sixty-four years that cheap hardboard suitcase had been my constant companion, a witness to all my struggles, my successes, my failures, my follies.

'No, we can't throw it away,' I said, 'Put it in the attic, fill it with all those pastries I'm not supposed to eat, and let the mice make merry!'

HANGING AT THE MANGO TAPE

The two captive policemen, Inspector Hukam Singh and Sub-Inspector Guler Singh, were being pushed unceremoniously along the dusty, deserted, sun-drenched road. The people of the village had made themselves scarce. They would reappear only when the dacoits went away.

The leader of the dacoit gang was Mangal Singh Bundela, great-grandson of a Pindari adventurer who had been a thorn in the side of the British. Mangal was doing his best to be a thorn in the flesh of his own government. The local police force had been strengthened recently but it was still inadequate for dealing with the dacoits who knew the ravines better than any surveyor. The dacoit Mangal had made a fortune out of ransom. His chief victims were the sons of wealthy industrialists, moneylenders and landowners. But today, he had captured two police officials; of no value as far as ransom went, but prestigious prisoners who could be put to other uses...

Mangal Singh wanted to show off in front of the police. He would kill at least one of them—his reputation demanded it, but he would let the other go, in order that his legendary power and ruthlessness be given maximum publicity. A legend is always a help!

His red-and-green turban was tied rakishly to one side. His dhoti extended right down to his ankles. His slippers were embroidered with gold and silver thread. His weapon was not ancient matchlock but a well-greased .303 rifle. Two of his men had similar rifles. Some had revolvers. Only the smaller fry carried swords or country-made pistols. Mangal Singh's gang, though traditional in many ways, was up-to-date in the matter of weapons. Right now, they had the policemen's guns too.

'Come along, Inspector Sahib,' said Mangal Singh, in tones of police barbarity, tugging at the rope that encircled the stout Inspector's midriff. 'Had you captured me today, you would have been a hero. You would have taken all the credit even though you could not keep up with your men in the ravines. Too bad you chose to remain sitting in your jeep with the sub-inspector. The jeep will be useful to us. You will not. But I would like you to be a hero all the same and there is none better than a dead hero!' Mangal Singh's followers doubled up with laughter. They loved their leader's cruel sense of humour.

'As for you, Guler Singh,' he continued, giving his attention to the sub-inspector, 'you are a man from my own village. You should have joined me long ago. But you were never to be trusted. You thought there would he better pickings in the police, didn't you?'

Guler Singh said nothing, simply hung his head and wondered what his fate would be. He felt certain that Mangal Singh would devise some diabolical and fiendish method of dealing with his captives. Guler Singh's only hope was Constable Ghanshyam, who hadn't been caught by the dacoits because, at the time of the ambush, he had been in the bushes relieving himself.

'To the mango tope,' said Mangal Singh, prodding the policemen forward.

'Listen to me, Mangal,' said the perspiring inspector, who was ready to try anything to get out of his predicament. 'Let me go and I give you my word there'll be no trouble for you in this area as long as I am posted here. What could be more convenient than that?'

'Nothing,' said Mangal Singh. 'But your word isn't good. My word is different. I have told my men that I will hang you at the mango tope and I mean to keep my word. But I believe in fair play—I like a little sport! You may yet go free if your friend here, Sub-Inspector Guler Singh, has his wits about him.'

The inspector and his subordinate exchanged doubtful, puzzled looks. They were not to remain puzzled for long. On reaching the mango tope, the dacoits produced a good strong hempen rope, one end looped into a slip knot. Many a garland of marigolds had the inspector received during his mediocre career. Now, for the first time, he was being garlanded with a hangman's noose. He had seen hangings, he had rather enjoyed them, but he had no stomach for his own. The inspector begged for mercy. Who wouldn't have in his position?

'Be quiet,' commanded Mangal Singh. 'I do not want to know about your wife and your children and the manner in which they will starve. You shot my son last year.'

'Not I!' cried the inspector. 'It was some other.'

'You led the party. But now, just to show you that I'm a sporting fellow, I am going to have you strung up from this tree and then I am going to give Guler Singh six shots with a rifle, and if he can sever the rope that suspends you before you are dead, well then, you can remain alive and I will let you go! For your sake I hope the sub-inspector's aim is good. He will have to shoot fast. My man Phambiri, who has made this noose, was once the executioner in a city jail. He guarantees that you won't last more than fifteen seconds at the end of his rope.'

Guler Singh was taken to a spot about forty yards away. A rifle was thrust into his hands. Two dacoits clambered into the branches of the mango tree. The inspector, his hands tied behind, could only gaze at them in horror. His mouth opened and shut as though he already had need of more air. And then, suddenly, the rope went taut, up went the inspector, his throat caught in a vice, while the branch of the tree shook and mango blossoms fluttered to the ground. The inspector dangled from the rope, his feet about three feet above the ground.

'You can shoot,' said Mangal Singh, nodding to the sub-inspector.

And Guler Singh, his hands trembling a little, raised the rifle to his shoulder and fired three shots in rapid succession. But the rope was swinging violently and the inspector's body was jerking about like a fish on a hook. The bullets went wide.

Guler Singh found the magazine empty. He reloaded, wiped the stinging sweat from his eyes, raised the rifle again, took more careful aim. His hands were steadier now. He rested the sights on the upper portion of the rope, where there was less motion. Normally, he was a good shot but he had never been asked to demonstrate his skill in circumstances such as these.

The inspector still gyrated at the end of his rope. There was life in him yet. His face was purple. The world, in those choking moments, was a medley of upside-down roofs and a red sun spinning slowly towards him.

Guler Singh's rifle cracked again. An inch or two wide this time. But the fifth shot found its mark, sending small tuffs of rope winging into the air.

The shot did not sever the rope; it was only a nick.

Guler Singh had one shot left. He was quite calm. The

rifle sight followed the rope's swing, less agitated now that the inspector's convulsions were lessening. Guler Singh felt sure he could sever the rope this time.

And then, as his finger touched the trigger, an odd, disturbing thought slipped into his mind, stayed there, throbbing. 'Whose life are you trying to save? Hukam Singh has stood in the way of your promotion more than once. He had you chargesheeted for accepting fifty rupees from an unlicenced rickshaw-puller. He makes you do all the dirty work, blames you when things go wrong, takes the credit when there is credit to be taken. But for him, you'd be an inspector!'

The rope swayed slightly to the right. The rifle moved just a fraction to the left. The last shot rang out, clipping a sliver of bark from the mango tree.

The inspector was dead when they cut him down.

'Bad luck,' said Mangal Singh Bundela. 'You nearly saved him. But the next time I catch up with you, Guler Singh, it will be your turn to hang from the mango tree. So keep well away! You know that I am a man of my word. I keep it now by giving you your freedom.'

A few minutes later, the party of dacoits had melted away into the late afternoon shadows of the scrub forest. There was the sound of a jeep starting up. Then silence—a silence so profound that it seemed to be shouting in Guler Singh's ears.

As the village people began to trickle out of their houses, Constable Ghanshyam appeared as if from nowhere, swearing that he had lost his way in the jungle. Several people had seen the incident from their windows. They were unanimous in praising the sub-inspector for his brave attempt to save his superior's life. He had done his best.

'It is true,' thought Guler Singh. 'I did my best.'

That moment of hesitation before the last shot, the question that had suddenly reared up in the darkness of his mind, had already gone from his memory. We remember only what we want to remember.

'I did my best,' he told everyone.

And so he had.

THE CROOKED TREE

You must pass your exams and go to college, but do not feel that if you fail, you will be able to do nothing.

My room in Shahganj was very small. I had paced about in it so often that I knew its exact measurements: twelve feet by ten. The string of my cot needed tightening. The dip in the middle was so pronounced that I invariably woke up in the morning with a backache; but I was hopeless at tightening charpoy strings.

Under the cot was my tin trunk. Its contents ranged from old, rejected manuscripts to clothes and letters and photographs. I had resolved that one day, when I had made some money with a book, I would throw the trunk and everything else out of the window, and leave Shahganj forever. But until then, I was a prisoner. The rent was nominal, the window had a view of the bus stop and rickshaw stand, and I had nowhere else to go.

I did not live entirely alone. Sometimes a beggar spent the night on the balcony; and, during cold or wet weather, the boys from the tea shop, who normally slept on the pavement, crowded into the room.

Usually I woke early in the mornings, as sleep was fitful, uneasy, crowded with dreams. I knew it was five o'clock when

I heard the first upcountry bus leaving its shed. I would then get up and take a walk in the fields beyond the railroad tracks.

One morning, while I was walking in the fields, I noticed someone lying across the pathway, his head and shoulders hidden by the stalks of young sugar cane. When I came near, I saw he was a boy of about sixteen. His body was twitching convulsively, his face was very white, except where a little blood had trickled down his chin. His legs kept moving and his hands fluttered restlessly, helplessly.

'What's the matter with you?' I asked, kneeling down beside him.

But he was still unconscious and could not answer me.

I ran down the footpath to a well and, dipping the end of my shirt in a shallow trough of water, ran back and sponged the boy's face. The twitching ceased and, though he still breathed heavily, his hands became still and his face calm. He opened his eyes and stared at me without any immediate comprehension.

'You have bitten your tongue,' I said, wiping the blood from his mouth. 'Don't worry. I'll stay with you until you feel better.'

He sat up now and said, 'I'm all right, thank you.'

'What happened?' I asked, sitting down beside him.

'Oh, nothing much. It often happens, I don't know why. But I cannot control it.'

'Have you seen a doctor?'

'I went to the hospital in the beginning. They gave me some pills, which I had to take every day. But the pills made me so tired and sleepy that I couldn't work properly. So I stopped taking them. Now this happens once or twice a month. But what does it matter? I'm all right when it's over, and I don't feel anything while it is happening.'

He got to his feet, dusting his clothes and smiling at me.

He was slim, long-limbed and bony. There was a little fluff on his cheeks and the promise of a moustache.

'Where do you live?' I asked. 'I'll walk back with you.'

'I don't live anywhere,' he said. 'Sometimes I sleep in the temple, sometimes in the gurdwara. In summer months, I sleep in the municipal gardens.'

'Well, then let me come with you as far as the gardens.'

He told me that his name was Kamal, that he studied at the Shahganj High School, and that he hoped to pass his examinations in a few months' time. He was studying hard and, if he passed with a good division, he hoped to attend a college. If he failed, there was only the prospect of continuing to live in the municipal gardens...

He carried with him a small tray of merchandise, supported by straps that went round his shoulders. In it were combs and buttons and cheap toys and little vials of perfume. All day, he walked about Shahganj, selling odds and ends to people in the bazaar or at their houses. He made, on an average, two rupees a day, which was enough for his food and his school fees.

He told me all this while we walked back to the bus stand. I returned to my room, to try and write something, while Kamal went on to the bazaar to try and sell his wares.

There was nothing very unusual about Kamal's being an orphan and a refugee. During the communal holocaust of 1947, thousands of homes had been broken up, and women and children had been killed. What was unusual in Kamal was his sensitivity, a quality I thought rare in a Punjabi youth who had grown up in the Frontier Provinces during a period of hate and violence. And it was not so much his positive attitude to life that appealed to me (most people in Shahganj were completely resigned to their lot) as his gentleness, his quiet voice and the smile that flickered across his face regardless of whether he was sad or happy. In the morning, when I opened my door, I found Kamal asleep at the top of the steps. His tray lay a few feet away. I shook him gently, and he woke at once.

'Have you been sleeping here all night?' I asked. 'Why didn't you come inside?'

'It was very late,' he said. 'I didn't want to disturb you.'

'Someone could have stolen your things while you slept.'

'Oh, I sleep quite lightly. Besides, I have nothing of special value. But I came to ask you something.'

'Do you need any money?'

'No. I want you to take your meal with me tonight.'

'But where? You don't have a place of your own. It will be too expensive in a restaurant.'

'In your room,' said Kamal. 'I will bring the food and cook it here. You have a stove?'

'I think so,' I said. 'I will have to look for it.'

'I will come at seven,' said Kamal, strapping on his tray. 'Don't worry. I know how to cook!'

He ran down the steps and made for the bazaar. I began to look for the oil stove, found it at the bottom of my tin trunk, and then discovered I hadn't any pots or pans or dishes. Finally, I borrowed these from Deep Chand, the barber.

Kamal brought a chicken for our dinner. This was a costly luxury in Shahganj, to be taken only two or three times a year. He had bought the bird for three rupees, which was cheap, considering it was not too skinny. While Kamal set about roasting it, I went down to the bazaar and procured a bottle of beer on credit, and this served as an appetizer.

'We are having an expensive meal,' I observed. 'Three rupees for the chicken and three rupees for the beer. But I wish we could do it more often.'

'We should do it at least once a month,' said Kamal. 'It should be possible if we work hard.'

'You know how to work. You work from morning to night.'

'But you are a writer, Rusty. That is different. You have to wait for a mood.'

'Oh, I'm not a genius that I can afford the luxury of moods. No, I'm just lazy, that's all.'

'Perhaps you are writing the wrong things.'

'I know I am. But I don't know how I can write anything else.'

'Have you tried?'

'Yes, but there is no money in it. I wish I could make a living in some other way. Even if I repaired cycles, I would make more money.'

'Then why not repair cycles?'

'No, I will not repair cycles. I would rather be a bad writer than a good repairer of cycles. But let us not think of work. There is time enough for work. I want to know more about you.'

Kamal did not know if his parents were alive or dead. He had lost them, literally, when he was six. It happened at the Amritsar railroad station, where trains coming across the border disgorged thousands of refugees, or pulled into the station half empty, drenched with blood and littered with corpses.

Kamal and his parents were lucky to escape the massacre. Had they travelled on an earlier train (they had tried desperately to get into one), they might well have been killed; but circumstances favoured them then, only to trick them later.

Kamal was clinging to his mother's sari, while she remained close to her husband, who was elbowing his way through the frightened, bewildered throng of refugees. Glancing over his shoulder at a woman who lay on the ground, wailing and beating her breasts, Kamal collided with a burly Sikh and lost his grip on his mother's sari.

The Sikh had a long curved sword at his waist; and Kamal stared up at him in awe and fascination—at his long hair, which had fallen loose, and his wild black beard, and the bloodstains on his white shirt. The Sikh pushed him out of the way and when Kamal looked around for his mother, she was not to be seen. She was hidden from him by a mass of restless bodies, pushed in different directions. He could hear her calling, 'Kamal, where are you, Kamal?' He tried to force his way through the crowd, in the direction of the voice, but he was carried the other way...

At night, when the platform was empty, he was still searching for his mother. Eventually, some soldiers took him away. They looked for his parents, but without success, and finally, they sent Kamal to a refugee camp. From there he went to an orphanage. But when he was eight, and felt himself a man, he ran away.

He worked for some time as a helper in a tea shop; but, when he started getting epileptic fits, the shopkeeper asked him to leave, and he found himself on the streets, begging for a living. He begged for a year, moving from one town to another, and ended up finally at Shahganj. By then, he was twelve and too old to beg; but he had saved some money, and with it he bought a small stock of combs, buttons, cheap perfumes and bangles; and, converting himself into a mobile shop, went from door to door, selling his wares.

Shahganj was a small town, and there was no house which Kamal hadn't visited. Everyone recognized him, and there were some who offered him food and drink; the children knew him well, because he played a small flute whenever he made his rounds, and they followed him to listen to the flute.

I began to look forward to Kamal's presence. He dispelled some of my own loneliness. I found I could work better, knowing that I did not have to work alone. And Kamal came to me, perhaps because I was the first person to have taken a personal interest in his life, and because I saw nothing frightening in his sickness. Most people in Shahganj thought epilepsy was infectious; some considered it a form of divine punishment for sins committed in a former life. Except for children, those who knew of his condition generally gave him a wide berth.

At sixteen, a boy grows like young wheat, springing up so fast that he is unaware of what is taking place within him. His mind quickens, his gestures become more confident. Hair sprouts like young grass on his face and chest, and his muscles begin to mature. Never again will he experience so much change and growth in so short a time. He is full of currents and countercurrents.

Kamal combined the bloom of youth with the beauty of the short-lived. It made me sad even to look at his pale, slim body. It hurt me to look into his eyes. Life and death were always struggling in their depths.

'Should I go to Delhi and take up a job?' I asked.

'Why not? You are always talking about it.'

'Why don't you come, too? Perhaps they can stop your fits.'

'We will need money for that. When I have passed my examinations, I will come.'

'Then I will wait,' I said. I was twenty-two, and there was world enough and time for everything.

We decided to save a little money from his small earnings and my occasional payments. We would need money to go to Delhi, money to live there until we could earn a living. We put away twenty rupees one week, but lost it the next when we lent it to a friend who owned a cycle rickshaw. But this gave us the occasional use of his cycle rickshaw, and early one morning, with Kamal sitting on the crossbar, I rode out of Shahganj.

After cycling for about two miles, we got down and pushed the cycle off the road, taking a path through a paddy field and then through a field of young maize, until, in the distance, we saw a tree, a crooked tree, growing beside an old well.

I do not know the name of that tree. I had never seen one like it before. It had a crooked trunk and crooked branches, and was clothed in thick, broad, crooked leaves, like the leaves on which food is served in the bazaar.

In the trunk of the tree there was a hole, and when we set the bicycle down with a crash, a pair of green parrots flew out, and went dipping and swerving across the fields. There was grass around the well, cropped short by grazing cattle.

We sat in the shade of the crooked tree, and Kamal untied the red cloth in which he had brought our food. When we had eaten, we stretched ourselves out on the grass. I closed my eyes and became aware of a score of different sensations. I heard a cricket singing in the tree, the cooing of pigeons from the walls of the old well, the quiet breathing of Kamal, the parrots returning to the tree, the distant hum of an airplane. I smelled the grass and the old bricks round the well and the promise of rain. I felt Kamal's fingers against my arm, and the sun creeping over my cheek. And when I opened my eyes, there were clouds on the horizon, and Kamal was asleep, his arm thrown across his face to keep out the glare.

I went to the well, and putting my shoulders to the ancient handle, turned the wheel, moving it around while cool, clean water gushed out over the stones and along the channel to the fields. The discovery that I could water a field, that I had the power to make things grow, gave me a thrill of satisfaction; it was like writing a story that had the ring of truth. I drank from one of the trays; the water was sweet with age.

Kamal was sitting up, looking at the sky.

'It's going to rain,' he said.

We began cycling homeward; but we were still some way out of Shahganj when it began to rain. A lashing wind swept the rain across our faces, but we exulted in it, and sang at the top of our voices until we reached the Shahganj bus stop.

Across the railroad tracks and the dry riverbed, fields of maize stretched away, until there came a dry region of thorn bushes and lantana scrub, where the earth was cut into jagged cracks, like a jigsaw puzzle. Dotting the landscape were old, abandoned brick kilns. When it rained heavily, the hollows filled up with water.

Kamal and I came to one of these hollows to bathe and swim. There was an island in the middle of it, and on this small mound lay the ruins of a hut where a nightwatchman had once lived, looking after the brick kilns. We would swim out to the island, which was only a few yards from the banks of the hollow. There was a grassy patch in front of the hut, and early in the mornings, before it got too hot, we would wrestle on the grass.

Though I was heavier than Kamal, my chest as sound as a new drum, he had strong, wiry arms and legs, and would often pinion me around the waist with his bony knees. Now, while we wrestled on the new monsoon grass, I felt his body go tense. He stiffened, his legs jerked against my body, and a shudder passed through him. I knew that he had a fit coming on, but I was unable to extricate myself from his arms.

He gripped me more tightly as the fit took possession of him. Instead of struggling, I lay still, tried to absorb some of his anguish, tried to draw some of his agitation to myself. I had a strange fancy that by identifying myself with his convulsions, I might alleviate them.

I pressed against Kamal, and whispered soothingly into his ear; and then, when I noticed his mouth working, I thrust my fingers between his teeth to prevent him from biting his tongue. But so violent was the convulsion that his teeth bit into the flesh of my palm and ground against my knuckles. I shouted with the pain and tried to jerk my hand away, but it was impossible to loosen the grip of his jaws. So I closed my eyes and counted—counted till seven—until consciousness returned to him and his muscles relaxed.

My hand was shaking and covered with blood. I bound it in my handkerchief and kept it hidden from Kamal.

We walked back to the room without talking much. Kamal looked depressed and weak. I kept my hand beneath my shirt, and Kamal was too dejected to notice anything. It was only at night, when he returned from his classes, that he noticed the cuts, and I told him I had slipped in the road, cutting my hand on some broken glass.

Rain upon Shahganj. And, until the rain stops, Shahganj is fresh and clean and alive. The children run out of their houses, glorying in their nakedness. The gutters choke, and the narrow street becomes a torrent of water, coursing merrily down to the bus stop. It swirls over the trees and the roofs of the town, and the parched earth soaks it up, exuding a fragrance that comes only once in a year, the fragrance of quenched earth, that most exhilarating of smells.

The rain swept in through the door and soaked the cot.

When I had succeeded in closing the door, I found the roof leaking, the water trickling down the walls and forming new pictures on the cracking plaster. The door flew open again, and there was Kamal standing on the threshold, shaking himself like a wet dog. Coming in, he stripped and dried himself, and then sat shivering on the bed while I made frantic efforts to close the door again.

'You need some tea,' I said.

He nodded, forgetting to smile for once, and I knew his mind was elsewhere, in one of a hundred possible places from his dreams.

'One day I will write a book,' I said, as we drank strong tea in the fast-fading twilight. 'A real book, about real people. Perhaps it will be about you and me and Shahganj. And then we will run away from Shahganj, fly on the wings of Garuda, and all our troubles will be over and fresh troubles will begin. Why should we mind difficulties, as long as they are new difficulties?'

'First, I must pass my exams,' said Kamal. 'Otherwise, I can do nothing, go nowhere.'

'Don't take exams too seriously. I know that in India they are the passport to any kind of job, and that you cannot become a clerk unless you have a degree. But do not forget that you are studying for the sake of acquiring knowledge, and not for the sake of becoming a clerk. You don't want to become a clerk or a bus conductor, do you? You must pass your exams and go to college, but do not feel that if you fail, you will be able to do nothing. Why, you can start making your own buttons instead of selling other people's!'

'You are right,' said Kamal. 'But why not be an educated button manufacturer?'

'Why not, indeed? That's just what I mean. And, while

you are studying for your exams, I will be writing my book. I will start tonight! It is an auspicious night, the beginning of the monsoon.'

The light did not come on. A tree must have fallen across the wires. I lit a candle and placed it on the windowsill and, while the candle spluttered in the steamy air, Kamal opened his books and, with one hand on a book and the other hand playing with his toes—this attitude helped him to concentrate—he devoted his attention to algebra.

I took an ink bottle down from a shelf and, finding it empty, added a little rainwater to the crusted contents. Then I sat down beside Kamal and began to write; but the pen was useless and made blotches all over the paper, and I had no idea what I should write about, though I was full of writing just then. So I began to look at Kamal instead; at his eyes, hidden in shadow, and his hands, quiet in the candlelight; and I followed his breathing and the slight movement of his lips as he read softly to himself.

And, instead of starting my book, I sat and watched Kamal.

Sometimes Kamal played the flute at night, while I was lying awake; and, even when I was asleep, the flute would play in my dreams. Sometimes he brought it to the crooked tree, and played it for the benefit of the birds; but the parrots only made harsh noises and flew away.

Once, when Kamal was playing his flute to a group of children, he had a fit. The flute fell from his hands, and he began to roll about in the dust on the roadside. The children were frightened and ran away. But the next time they heard Kamal play his flute, they came to listen as usual.

That Kamal was gaining in strength, I knew from the way he was able to pin me down whenever we wrestled on the grass near the old brick kilns. It was no longer necessary for me to yield deliberately to him. And, though his fits still recurred from time to time—as we knew they would continue to do—he was not so depressed afterwards. The anxiety and the death had gone from his eyes.

His examinations were nearing, and he was working hard. (I had yet to begin the first chapter of my book.) Because of the necessity of selling two or three rupees' worth of articles every day, he did not get much time for studying; but he stuck to his books until past midnight, and it was seldom that I heard his flute.

He put aside his tray of odds and ends during the examinations, and walked to the examination centre instead. And after two weeks, when it was all over, he took up his tray and began his rounds again. In a burst of creativity, I wrote three pages of my novel.

On the morning the results of the examination were due, I rose early, before Kamal, and went down to the news agency. It was five o'clock and the newspapers had just arrived. I went through the columns relating to Shahganj, but I couldn't find Kamal's roll number on the list of successful candidates. I had the number written down on a slip of paper, and I looked at it again to make sure that I had compared it correctly with the others; then I went through the newspaper once more.

When I returned to the room, Kamal was sitting on the doorstep. I didn't have to tell him he had failed. He knew by the look on my face. I sat down beside him, and we said nothing for some time.

'Never mind,' said Kamal, eventually. 'I will pass next year.'

I realized that I was more depressed than he was, and that he was trying to console me.

'If only you'd had more time,' I said.

'I have plenty of time now. Another year. And you will have time in which to finish your book; then we can both go away. Another year of Shahganj won't be so bad. As long as I have your friendship, almost everything else can be tolerated, even my sickness.'

And then, turning to me with an expression of intense happiness, he said, 'Yesterday I was sad, and tomorrow I may be sad again, but today I know that I am happy. I want to live on and on. I feel that life isn't long enough to satisfy me.'

He stood up, the tray hanging from his shoulders.

'What would you like to buy?' he said. 'I have everything you need.'

At the bottom of the steps he turned and smiled at me, and I knew then that I had written my story.

ESCAPE FROM JAVA

It all happened within the space of a few days. The Cassia tree had barely come into flower when the first bombs fell on Batavia (now called Jakarta) and the bright pink blossoms lay scattered over the wreckage in the streets.

News had reached us that Singapore had fallen to the Japanese. My father said, 'I expect it won't be long before they take Java. With the British defeated, how can the Dutch be expected to win!' He did not mean to be critical of the Dutch; he knew they did not have the backing of the Empire that Britain had, Singapore had been called the Gibraltar of the East. After its surrender there could only be retreat, a vast exodus of Europeans from southeast Asia.

It was the Second World War. What the Javanese thought about the war is now hard for me to say, because I was only nine at the time and knew very little of worldly matters. Most people knew they would be exchanging their Dutch rulers for Japanese rulers; but there were also many who spoke in terms of freedom for Java when the war was over.

Our neighbour, Mr Hartono, was one of those who looked ahead to a time when Java, Sumatra and the other islands would make up one independent nation. He was a college professor and spoke Dutch, Chinese, Javanese and a little English. His son, Sono, was about my age. He was the only boy I knew who could talk to me in English, and as a result we spent a lot of time together. Our favourite pastime was flying kites in the park.

The bombing soon put an end to kite flying. Air raid alerts sounded at all hours of the day and night and, although in the beginning most of the bombs fell near the docks, a couple of miles from where we lived, we had to stay indoors. If the planes sounded very near, we dived under beds or tables. I don't remember if there were any trenches. Probably there hadn't been time for trench digging, and now, there was time only for digging graves. Events had moved all too swiftly, and everyone (except, of course, the Javanese) was anxious to get away from Java.

'When are you going?' asked Sono, as we sat on the verandah steps in a pause between air raids.

'I don't know,' I said. 'It all depends on my father.'

'My father says the Japs will be here in a week. And if you're still here then, they'll put you to work building a railway.'

'I wouldn't mind building a railway,' I said.

'But they won't give you enough to eat. Just rice with worms in it. And if you don't work properly, they'll shoot you.'

'They do that to soldiers,' I said. 'We're civilians.'

'They do it to civilians, too,' said Sono.

What were my father and I doing in Batavia, when our home had been first in India and then in Singapore? He worked for a firm dealing in rubber, and six months earlier he had been sent to Batavia to open a new office in partnership with a Dutch business house. Although I was so young, I accompanied my father almost everywhere. My mother left when I was very small, and my father had always looked after me. After the war was over, he was going to take me to England.

'Are we going to win the war?' I asked.

'It doesn't look it from here,' he said.

No, it didn't look as though we were winning. Standing at the docks with my father, I watched the ships arrive from Singapore crowded with refugees—men, women and children, all living on the decks in the hot tropical sun; they looked pale and worn out and worried. They were on their way to Colombo or Bombay. No one came ashore at Batavia. It wasn't British territory; it was Dutch, and everyone knew it wouldn't be Dutch for long.

'Aren't we going too?' I asked. 'Sono's father says the Japs will be here any day.'

'We've still got a few days,' said my father. He was a short, stocky man who seldom got excited. If he was worried, he didn't show it. 'I've got to wind up a few business matters, and then we'll be off.'

'How will we go? There's no room for us on those ships.'

'There certainly isn't. But we'll find a way, lad, don't worry.'

I didn't worry. I had complete confidence in my father's ability to find a way out of difficulties. He used to say, 'Every problem has a solution hidden away somewhere, and if only you look hard enough you will find it.'

There were British soldiers in the streets but they did not make it feel much safer. They were just waiting for troop ships to come and take them away. No one, it seemed, was interested in defending Java, only in getting out as fast as possible.

Although the Dutch were unpopular with the Javanese people, there was no ill-feeling against individual Europeans. I could walk safely through the streets. Occasionally, small boys in the crowded Chinese quarter would point at me and shout, '*Orang Balandi!*' (Dutchman!) But they did so in good burnout, and I didn't know the language well enough to stop and explain that the English weren't Dutch. For them, all white people were the same, and understandably so.

My father's office was in the commercial area, along the canal banks. Our two-storeyed house, about a mile away, was an old building with a roof of red tiles and a broad balcony which had stone dragons at either end. There were flowers in the garden almost all the year round. If there was anything in Batavia more regular than the bombing, it was the rain, which came pattering down on the roof and on the banana fronds almost every afternoon. In the hot and steamy atmosphere of Java, the rain was always welcome.

There were no anti-aircraft guns in Batavia—at least we never heard any—and the Jap bombers came over at will, dropping their bombs by daylight. Sometimes bombs fell in the town. One day, the building next to my father's office received a direct lilt and tumbled into the river. A number of office workers were killed.

The schools closed, and Sono and I had nothing to do all day except sit in the house, playing darts or carrom, wrestling on the carpets, or playing the gramophone. We had records by Gracie Fields, Harry Lauder, George Formby and Arthur Askey, all popular British artists of the early 1940s. One song by Arthur Askey made fun of Adolf Hitler, with the words, 'Adolf, we're gonna hang up your washing on the Siegfried Line, if the Siegfried Line's still there!' It made us feel quite cheerful to know that back in Britain people were confident of winning the war!

One day, Sono said, 'The bombs are falling on Batavia, not in the countryside. Why don't we get cycles and ride out of town?'

I fell in with the idea at once. After the morning all-clear had sounded, we mounted our cycles and rode out of town. Mine was a hired cycle, but Sono's was his own. He'd had it since the age of five, and it was constantly in need of repair. 'The soul has gone out of it,' he used to say.

Our fathers were at work; Sono's mother had gone out to do her shopping (during air raids she took shelter under the most convenient shop counter) and wouldn't be back for at least an hour. We expected to be back before lunch.

We were soon out of town, on a road that passed through rice fields, pineapple orchards and cinchona plantations. On our right lay dark green hills; on our left, groves of coconut palms and, beyond them, the sea. Men and women were working in the rice fields, knee-deep in mud, their broad-brimmed hats protecting them from the fierce sun. Here and there, a buffalo wallowed in a pool of brown water, while a naked boy lay stretched out on the animal's broad back.

We took a bumpy track through the palms. They grew right down to the edge of the sea. Leaving our cycles on the shingle, we ran down a smooth, sandy beach and into the shallow water.

'Don't go too far in,' warned Sono. 'There may be sharks about.'

Wading in amongst the rocks, we searched for interesting shells, then sat clown on a large rock and looked out to sea, where a sailing ship moved placidly on the crisp, blue waters. It was difficult to imagine that half the world was at war, and that Batavia, two or three miles away, was right in the middle of it.

On our way home, we decided to take a short cut through the rice fields, but soon found that our tyres got bogged down in the soft mud. This delayed our return; and to make things worse, we got the roads mixed up and reached an area of the town that seemed unfamiliar. We had barely entered the outskirts when the siren sounded, followed soon after by the drone of approaching aircraft.

'Should we get off our cycles and take shelter somewhere?' I called out.

'No, let's race home!' shouted Sono. 'The bombs won't fall here.'

But he was wrong. The planes flew in very low. Looking up for a moment, I saw the sun blotted out by the sinister shape of a Jap fighter-bomber. We pedalled furiously; but we had barely covered fifty yards when there was a terrific explosion on our right, behind some houses. The shock sent us spinning across the road. We were flung from our cycles. And the cycles, still propelled by the blast, crashed into a wall.

I felt a stinging sensation in my hands and legs, as though scores of little insects had bitten me. Tiny droplets of blood appeared here and there on my flesh. Sono was on all fours, crawling beside me, and I saw that he too had the same small scratches on his hands and forehead, made by tiny shards of flying glass. We were quickly on our feet, and then we began running in the general direction of our homes. The twisted cycles lay forgotten on the road.

'Get off the street, you two!' shouted someone from a window; but we weren't going to stop running until we got home. And we ran faster than we'd ever run in our lives.

My father and Sono's parents were themselves running about the street, calling for us, when we came rushing around the corner and tumbled into their arms.

'Where have you been?'

'What happened to you?'

'How did you get those cuts?'

All superfluous questions but before we could recover our breath and start explaining, we were bundled into our respective homes. My father washed my cuts and scratches, dabbed at my face and legs with iodine—ignoring my yelps—and then stuck plaster all over my face.

Sono and I had had a fright, and we did not venture far from the house again.

That night, my father said: 'I think we'll be able to leave in a day or two.'

'Has another ship come in?'

'No.'

'Then how are we going? By plane?'

'Wait and see, lad. It isn't settled yet. But we won't be able to take much with us—just enough to fill a couple of travelling bags.'

'What about the stamp collection?' I asked.

My father's stamp collection was quite valuable and filled several volumes.

'I'm afraid we'll have to leave most of it behind,' he said. 'Perhaps Mr Hartono will keep it for me, and when the war is over—if it's over—we'll come back for it.'

'But we can take one or two albums with us, can't we?'

'I'll take one. There'll be room for one. Then if we're short of money in Bombay, we can sell the stamps.'

'Bombay? That's in India. I thought we were going back to England.'

'First, we must go to India.'

The following morning I found Sono in the garden, patched up like me, and with one foot in a bandage. But he was as cheerful as ever and gave me his usual wide grin.

'We're leaving tomorrow,' I said.

The grin left his face.

'I will be sad when you go,' he said. 'But I will he glad too, because then you will be able to escape from the Japs.'

'After the war, I'll come back.'

'Yes, you must come back. And then, when we are big, we will go round the world together. I want to see England and America and Africa and India and Japan. I want to go everywhere.'

'We can't go everywhere.'

'Yes, we can. No one can stop us!'

We had to be up very early the next morning. Our bags had been packed late at night. We were taking a few clothes, some of my father's business papers, a pair of binoculars, one stamp album, and several bars of chocolate. I was pleased about the stamp album and the chocolates, but I had to give up several of my treasures—favourite books, the gramophone and records, an old Samurai sword, a train set and a dartboard. The only consolation was that Sono, and not a stranger, would have them. In the first faint light of dawn, a truck drew up in front of the house. It was driven by a Dutch businessman, Mr Hookens, who worked with my father. Sono was already at the gate, waiting to say goodbye.

'I have a present for you,' he said.

He took me by the hand and pressed a smooth hard object into my palm. I grasped it and then held it up against the light. It was a beautiful little seahorse, carved out of pale blue jade.

'It will bring you luck,' said Sono.

'Thank you,' I said. 'I will keep it forever.'

And I slipped the little seahorse into my pocket.

'In you get, lad,' said my father, and I got up on the front seat between him and Mr Hookens.

As the truck started up, I turned to wave to Sono. He was sitting on his garden wall, grinning at me. He called out: 'We will go everywhere, and no one can stop us!'

He was still waving when the truck took us round the bend at the end of the road.

We drove through the still, quiet streets of Batavia, occasionally passing burnt-out trucks and shattered buildings. Then we left the sleeping city far behind and were climbing into the forested hills. It had rained during the night, and when the sun came up over the green hills, it twinkled and glittered on the broad, wet leaves. The light in the forest changed from dark green to greenish gold, broken here and there by the flaming red or orange of a trumpet-shaped blossom. It was impossible to know the names of all those fantastic plants! The road had been cut through dense tropical forest, and on either side the trees jostled each other, hungry for the sun; but they were chained together by the liana creepers and vines that fed upon the struggling trees.

Occasionally, a jelarang, a large Javan squirrel, frightened by the passing of the truck, leapt through the trees before disappearing into the depths of the forest. We saw many birds: peacocks, junglefowl, and once, standing majestically at the side of the road, a crowned pigeon, its great size and splendid crest making it a striking object even at a distance. Mr Hookens slowed down so that we could look at the bird. It bowed its head so that its crest swept the ground; then it emitted a low hollow boom rather than the call of a turkey.

When we came to a small clearing, we stopped for breakfast. Butterflies, black, green and gold, flitted across the clearing. The silence of the forest was broken only by the drone of airplanes. Japanese Zeros heading for Batavia on another raid. I thought about Sono, and wondered what he would be doing at home: probably trying out the gramophone!

We ate boiled eggs and drank tea from a thermos, then got back into the truck and resumed our journey.

I must have dozed off soon after, because the next thing I remember is that we were going quite fast down a steep, winding road, and in the distance I could see a calm blue lagoon.

'We've reached the sea again,' I said.

'That's right,' said my father. 'But we're now nearly a hundred miles from Batavia, in another part of the island. You're looking out over the Sunda Straits.'

Then he pointed towards a shimmering white object resting on the waters of the lagoon.

'There's our plane,' he said.

'A seaplane!' I exclaimed. 'I never guessed. Where will it take us?'

'To Bombay, I hope. There aren't many other places left to go to!'

It was a very old seaplane, and no one, not even the captain— the pilot was called the captain—could promise that it would take off. Mr Hookens wasn't coming with us; he said the plane would be back for him the next day. Besides my father and me, there were four other passengers, and all but one were Dutch. The odd man out was a Londoner, a motor mechanic who'd been left behind in Java when his unit was evacuated. (He told us later that he'd fallen asleep at a bar in the Chinese quarter, waking up some hours after his regiment had moved off!) He looked rather scruffy. He'd lost the top button of his shirt, but, instead of leaving his collar open, as we did, he'd kept it together with a large safety pin, which thrust itself out from behind a bright pink tie.

'It's a relief to find you here, guvnor,' he said, shaking my father by the hand. 'Knew you for a Yorkshireman the minute I set eyes on you. It's the song-fried that does it, if you know what I mean.' (He meant 'sangfroid', French for a 'cool look'.) 'And here I was, with all these flippin' forriners, and me not knowing a word of what they've been yattering about. Do you think this old tub will get us back to Blighty?'

'It does look a bit shaky,' said my father. 'One of the first flying boats, from the looks of it. If it gets us to Bombay, that's far enough.'

'Anywhere out of Java's good enough for me,' said our new companion. 'The name's Muggeridge.'

'Pleased to know you, Mr Muggeridge,' said my father. 'I'm Bond. This is my son.'

Mr Muggeridge rumpled my hair and favoured me with a large wink.

The captain of the seaplane was beckoning to us to join him in a small skiff which was about to take us across a short stretch of water to the seaplane.

'Here we go,' said Mr Muggeridge. 'Say your prayers and keep your fingers crossed.'

The seaplane took a long time getting airborne. It had to make several runs before it finally took off. Then, lurching drunkenly, it rose into the clear blue sky.

'For a moment I thought we were going to end up in the briny,' said Mr Muggeridge, untying his seat belt. 'And talkin' of fish, I'd give a week's wages for a plate of fish an' chips and a pint of beer.'

'I'll buy you a beer in Bombay,' said my father.

'Have an egg,' I said, remembering we still had some boiled eggs in one of the travelling bags.

'Thanks, mate,' said Mr Muggeridge, accepting an egg with alacrity. 'A real egg, too! I've been livin' on egg powder these last six months. That's what they give you in the army. And it ain't hens' eggs they make it from, let me tell you. It's either gulls' or turtles' eggs!'

'No,' said my father with a straight face. 'Snakes' eggs.'

Mr Muggeridge turned a delicate shade of green; but he soon recovered his poise, and for about an hour kept talking about almost everything under the sun, including Churchill, Hitler, Roosevelt, Mahatma Gandhi, and Betty Grable. (The last-named was famous for her beautiful legs.) He would have gone on talking all the way to Bombay had he been given a chance; but suddenly a shudder passed through the old plane, and it began lurching again.

'I think an engine is giving trouble,' said my father.

When I looked through the small glassed-in window, it seemed as though the sea was rushing up to meet us.

The co-pilot entered the passenger cabin and said something in Dutch. The passengers looked dismayed, and immediately began fastening their seat belts.

'Well, what did the blighter say?' asked Mr Muggeridge.

'I think he's going to have to ditch the plane,' said my father, who knew enough Dutch to get the gist of anything that was said.

'Down in the drink!' exclaimed Mr Muggeridge. 'Gawd, 'elp us! And how far are we from Bombay, guy?'

'A few hundred miles,' said my father.

'Can you swim, mate?' asked Mr Muggeridge looking at me.

'Yes,' I said. 'But not all the way to Bombay. How far can you swim?'

'The length of a bathtub,' he said.

'Don't worry,' said my father. 'Just make sure your life jacket's properly tied.'

We looked to our life jackets; my father checked mine twice, making sure that it was properly fastened.

The pilot had now cut both engines, and was bringing the plane down in a circling movement. But he couldn't control the speed, and it was tilting heavily to one side. Instead of landing smoothly on its belly, it came down on a wing tip, and this caused the plane to swivel violently around in the choppy sea. There was a terrific jolt when the plane hit the water, and if it hadn't been for the seat belts, we'd have been flung from our seats. Even so, Mr Muggeridge struck his head against the seat in front, and he was now holding a bleeding nose and using some shocking language.

As soon as the plane came to a standstill, my father undid my seat belt. There was no time to lose. Water was already filling the cabin, and all the passengers—except one, who was dead in his seat with a broken neck—were scrambling for the exit hatch. The co-pilot pulled a lever and the door fell away to reveal high waves slapping against the sides of the stricken plane.

Holding me by the hand, my father was leading me towards the exit.

'Quick, lad,' he said. 'We won't stay afloat for long.'

'Give us a hand!' shouted Mr Muggeridge, still struggling with his life jacket. 'First this bloody bleedin' nose, and now something's gone and stuck.'

My father helped him fix the life jacket, then pushed him out of the door ahead of us.

As we swam away from the seaplane (Mr Muggeridge splashing fiercely alongside us), we were aware of the other passengers in the water. One of them shouted to us in Dutch to follow him.

We swam after him towards the dinghy, which had been released the moment we hit the water. That yellow dinghy, bobbing about on the waves, was as welcome as land.

All who had left the plane managed to climb into the dinghy. We were seven altogether—a tight fit. We had hardly settled down in the well of the dinghy when Mr Muggeridge, still holding his nose, exclaimed: 'There she goes!' And as we looked on helplessly, the seaplane sank swiftly and silently beneath the waves.

The dinghy had shipped a lot of water, and soon everyone was busy bailing it out with mugs (there were a couple in the dinghy), hats, and bare hands. There was a light swell, and every now and then, water would roll in again and half fill the dinghy. But within half an hour, we had most of the water out, and then it was possible to take turns, two men doing the bailing while the others rested. No one expected me to do this work, but I gave a hand anyway, using my father's sola topi for the purpose.

'Where are we?' asked one of the passengers.

'A long way from anywhere,' said another.

'There must be a few islands in the Indian Ocean.'

'But we may be at sea for days before we come to one of them.'

'Days or even weeks,' said the captain. 'Let us look at our supplies.'

The dinghy appeared to be fairly well-provided with emergency rations: biscuits, raisins, chocolates (we'd lost our own), and enough water to last a week. There was also a first aid box, which was put to immediate use, as Mr Muggeridge's nose needed attention. A few others had cuts and bruises. One of the passengers had received a hard knock on the head and appeared to be suffering from a loss of memory. He had no idea how we happened to be drifting about in the middle of the Indian Ocean; he was convinced that we were on a pleasure cruise a few miles off Batavia.

The unfamiliar motion of the dinghy, as it rose and fell in the troughs between the waves, resulted in almost everyone getting seasick. As no one could eat anything, a day's rations were saved.

The sun was very hot, but my father covered my head with a large spotted handkerchief. He'd always had a fancy for bandana handkerchiefs with yellow spots, and seldom carried fewer than two on his person; so he had one for himself too. The sola topi, well-soaked in seawater, was being used by Mr Muggeridge.

It was only when I had recovered to some extent from my seasickness that I remembered the valuable stamp album, and sat up, exclaiming, 'The stamps! Did you bring the stamp album, Dad?'

He shook his head ruefully. 'It must be at the bottom of the sea by now,' he said. 'But don't worry, I kept a few rare stamps in my wallet.' And looking pleased with himself, he tapped the pocket of his hush shirt.

The dinghy drifted all day, with no one having the least idea where it might be taking us.

'Probably going round in circles,' said Mr Muggeridge pessimistically.

There was no compass and no sail, and paddling wouldn't have got us far even if we'd had paddles; we could only resign ourselves to the whims of the current and hope it would take us towards land or at least to within hailing distance of some passing ship.

The sun went down like an overripe tomato dissolving slowly in the sea. The darkness pressed down on us. It was a moonless night, and all we could see was the white foam on the crests of the waves. I lay with my head on my father's shoulder, and looked up at the stars which glittered in the remote heavens.

'Perhaps your friend Sono will look up at the sky tonight and see those same stars,' said my father. 'The world isn't so big after all.'

'All the same, there's a lot of sea around us,' said Mr Muggeridge from out of the darkness.

Remembering Sono, I put my hand in my pocket and was reassured to feel the smooth outline of the jade seahorse.

'I've still got Sono's seahorse,' I said, showing it to my father.

'Keep it carefully,' he said. 'It may bring us luck.'

'Are seahorses lucky?'

'Who knows? But he gave it to you with love, and love is like a prayer. So keep it carefully.'

I didn't sleep much that night. I don't think anyone slept. No one spoke much either, except, of course, Mr Muggeridge, who kept muttering something about cold beer and salami.

I didn't feel so sick the next day. By ten o'clock, I was quite hungry; but breakfast consisted of two biscuits, a piece of chocolate, and a little drinking water. It was another hot day, and we were soon very thirsty, but everyone agreed that we should ration ourselves strictly.

Two or three still felt ill, but the others, including Mr Muggeridge, had recovered their appetites and normal spirits, and there was some discussion about the prospects of being picked up.

'Are there any distress rockets in the dinghy?' asked my father. 'If we see a ship or a plane, we can fire a rocket and hope to be spotted. Otherwise there's not much chance of our being seen from a distance.'

A thorough search was made in the dinghy, but there were no rockets.

'Someone must have used them last Guy Fawkes Day,' commented Mr Muggeridge.

'They don't celebrate Guy Fawkes Day in Holland,' said my father. 'Guy Fawkes was an Englishman.'

'Ah,' said Mr Muggeridge, not in the least put out. 'I've always said, most great men are Englishmen. And what did this chap Guy Fawkes do?'

'Tried to blow up Parliament,' said my father.

That afternoon we saw our first sharks. They were enormous creatures, and as they glided backward and forward under the boat it seemed they might hit and capsize us. They went away for some time, but returned in the evening.

At night, as I lay half asleep beside my father, I felt a few drops of water strike my face. At first I thought it was the sea spray; but when the sprinkling continued, I realized that it was raining lightly.

'Rain!' I shouted, sitting up. 'It's raining!'

Everyone woke up and did his best to collect water in mugs, hats or other containers. Mr Muggeridge lay back with his mouth open, drinking the rain as it fell.

'This is more like it,' he said. 'You can have all the sun an' sand in the world. Give me a rainy day in England!'

But by early morning the clouds had passed, and the day turned out to be even hotter than the previous one. Soon we were all red and raw from sunburn. By midday, even Mr Muggeridge was silent. No one had the energy to talk.

Then my father whispered, 'Can you hear a plane, lad?'

I listened carefully, and above the hiss of the waves, I heard what sounded like the distant drone of a plane; it must have been very far away, because we could not see it. Perhaps it was flying into the sun, and the glare was too much for our sore eyes; or perhaps we'd just imagined the sound.

Then the Dutchman who'd lost his memory thought he saw land, and kept pointing towards the horizon and saying, 'That's Batavia, I told you, we were close to shore!' No one else saw anything. So my father and I weren't the only ones imagining things.

Said my father, 'It only goes to show that a man can see what he wants to see, even if there's nothing to be seen!'

The sharks were still with us. Mr Muggeridge began to resent them. He took off one of his shoes and hurled it at the nearest shark; but the big fish ignored the shoe and swam on after us.

'Now, if your leg had been in that shoe, Mr Muggeridge, the shark might have accepted it,' observed my father.

'Don't throw your shoes away,' said the captain. 'We might land on a deserted coastline and have to walk hundreds of miles!'

A light breeze sprang up that evening, and the dinghy moved more swiftly on the choppy water.

'At last we're moving forward,' said the captain.

'In circles,' said Mr Muggeridge.

But the breeze was refreshing; it cooled our burning limbs, and helped us to get some sleep. In the middle of the night, I woke up feeling very hungry.

'Are you all right?' asked my father, who had been awake all the time.

'Just hungry,' I said.

'And what would you like to eat?'

'Oranges!'

He laughed. 'No oranges on board. But I kept a piece of my chocolate for you. And there's a little water, if you're thirsty.' I kept the chocolate in my mouth for a long time, trying to make it last. Then I sipped a little water.

'Aren't you hungry?' I asked.

'Ravenous! I could eat a whole turkey. When we get to Bombay or Madras or Colombo, or wherever it is we get to, we'll go to the best restaurant in town and eat like-like—'

'Like shipwrecked sailors!' I said.

'Exactly.'

'Do you think we'll ever get to land, Dad?'

'I'm sure we will. You're not afraid, are you?'

'No. Not as long as you're with me.'

Next morning, to everyone's delight, we saw seagulls. This was a sure sign that land couldn't be far away; but a dinghy could take days to drift a distance of thirty or forty miles. The birds wheeled noisily above the dinghy. Their cries were the first familiar sounds we had heard for three days and three nights, apart from the wind and the sea and our own weary voices.

The sharks had disappeared, and that too was an encouraging sign. They didn't like the oil slicks that were appearing in the water.

But presently, the gulls left us, and we feared we were drifting away from land.

'Circles,' repeated Mr Muggeridge. 'Circles.'

We had sufficient food and water for another week at sea; but no one even wanted to think about spending another week at sea.

The sun was a ball of fire. Our water ration wasn't sufficient to quench our thirst. By noon, we were without much hope or energy.

My father had his pipe in his mouth. He didn't have any tobacco, but he liked holding the pipe between his teeth. He said it prevented his mouth from getting too dry.

The sharks came back.

Mr Muggeridge removed his other shoe and threw it at them.

'Nothing like a lovely wet English summer,' he mumbled.

I fell asleep in the well of the dinghy, my father's large handkerchief spread over my face. The yellow spots on the cloth seemed to grow into enormous revolving suns.

When I woke up, I found a huge shadow hanging over us. At first I thought it was a cloud. But it was a shifting shadow. My father took the handkerchief from my face and said, 'You can wake up now, lad. We'll be home and dry soon.'

A fishing boat was beside us, and the shadow came from its wide, flapping sail. A number of bronzed, smiling, chattering fishermen—Burmese, as we discovered later—were gazing down at us from the deck of their boat. A few days later, my father and I were in Bombay.

My father sold his rare stamps for over a thousand rupees, and we were able to live in a comfortable hotel. Mr Muggeridge was flown back to England. Later, we got a postcard from him saying the English rain was awful!

'And what about us?' I asked. 'Aren't we going back to England?'

'Not yet,' said my father. 'You'll be going to a boarding school in Simla, until the war's over.'

'But why should I leave you?' I asked.

'Because I've joined the RAF,' he said. 'Don't worry, I'm being posted to Delhi. I'll be able to come up to see you sometimes.'

A week later, I was on a small train which went chugging up the steep mountain track to Simla. Several Indian, Anglo-Indian and English children tumbled around in the compartment. I felt quite out of place among them, as though I had grown out of their pranks. But I wasn't unhappy. I knew my father would be coming to see me soon. He'd promised me some books, a pair of roller skates, and a cricket bat, just as soon as he got his first month's pay.

Meanwhile, I had the jade seahorse which Sono had given me.

And I have it with me today.

A JOB WELL DONE

Dhuki, the gardener, was clearing up the weeds that grew in profusion around the old disused well. He was an old man, skinny and bent and spindly-legged; but he had always been like that; his strength lay in his wrists and in his long, tendril-like fingers. He looked as frail as a petunia, but he had the tenacity of a vine.

'Are you going to cover the well?' I asked. I was eight, a great favourite of Dhuki. He had been the gardener long before my birth; had worked for my father, until my father died, and now worked for my mother and stepfather.

'I must cover it, I suppose,' said Dhuki. 'That's what the "Major sahib" wants. He'll be back any day, and if he finds the well still uncovered, he'll get into one of his raging fits and I'll be looking for another job!'

The 'Major sahib' was my stepfather, Major Summerskill. A tall, hearty, back-slapping man, who liked polo and pig-sticking. He was quite unlike my father. My father had always given me books to read. The Major said I would become a dreamer if I read too much, and took the books away. I hated him and did not think much of my mother for marrying him.

'The boy's too soft,' I heard him tell my mother. 'I must see that he gets riding lessons.'

But before the riding lessons could be arranged, the Major's regiment was ordered to Peshawar. Trouble was expected from some of the frontier tribes. He was away for about two months. Before leaving, he had left strict instructions for Dhuki to cover up the old well.

'Too damned dangerous having an open well in the middle of the garden,' my stepfather had said. 'Make sure that it's completely covered by the time I get back.'

Dhuki was loath to cover up the old well. It had been there for over fifty years, long before the house had been built. In its walls lived a colony of pigeons. Their soft cooing filled the garden with a lovely sound. And during the hot, dry, summer months, when taps ran dry, the well was always a dependable source of water. The bhisti still used it, filling his goatskin bag with the cool clear water and sprinkling the paths around the house to keep the dust down.

Dhuki pleaded with my mother to let him leave the well uncovered.

'What will happen to the pigeons?' he asked.

'Oh, surely they can find another well,' said my mother. 'Do close it up soon, Dhuki. I don't want the Sahib to come back and find that you haven't done anything about it.'

My mother seemed just a little bit afraid of the Major. How can we be afraid of those we love? It was a question that puzzled me then, and puzzles me still.

The Major's absence made life pleasant again. I returned to my books, spent long hours in my favourite banyan tree, ate buckets of mangoes, and dawdled in the garden talking to Dhuki.

Neither he nor I were looking forward to the Major's return. Dhuki had stayed on after my mother's second marriage only out of loyalty to her and affection for me; he had really been my father's man. But my mother had always appeared deceptively frail and helpless, and most men, Major Summerskill included, felt protective towards her. She liked people who did things for her.

'Your father liked this well,' said Dhuki. 'He would often sit here in the evenings, with a book in which he made drawings of birds and flowers and insects.'

I remembered those drawings, and I remembered how they had all been thrown away by the Major when he had moved into the house. Dhuki knew about it, too. I didn't keep much from him.

'It's a sad business closing this well,' said Dhuki again. 'Only a fool or a drunkard is likely to fall into it.'

But he had made his preparations. Planks of sal wood, bricks and cement were neatly piled up around the well.

'Tomorrow,' said Dhuki. 'Tomorrow I will do it. Not today. Let the birds remain for one more day. In the morning, Baba, you can help me drive the birds from the well.

On the day my stepfather was expected back, my mother hired a tonga and went to the bazaar to do some shopping. Only a few people had cars in those days. Even colonels went about in tongas. Now, a clerk finds it beneath his dignity to sit in one.

As the Major was not expected before evening, I decided I would make full use of my last free morning. I took all my favourite books and stored them away in an outhouse where I could come for them from time to time. Then, my pockets bursting with mangoes, I climbed into the banyan tree. It was the darkest and coolest place on a hot day in June.

From behind the screen of leaves that concealed me, I could see Dhuki moving about near the well. He appeared to be most unwilling to get on with the job of covering it up.

'Baba!' he called, several times; but I did not feel like stirring from the banyan tree. Dhuki grasped a long plank of wood and placed it across one end of the well. He started hammering. From my vantage point in the banyan tree, he looked very bent and old.

A jingle of tonga bells and the squeak of unoiled wheels told me that a tonga was coming in at the gate. It was too early for my mother to be back. I peered through the thick, waxy leaves of the tree, and nearly fell off my branch in surprise. It was my stepfather, the Major! He had arrived earlier than expected.

I did not come down from the tree. I had no intention of confronting my stepfather until my mother returned.

The Major had climbed down from the tonga and was watching his luggage being carried on to the verandah. He was red in the face and the ends of his handlebar moustache were stiff with brilliantine. Dhuki approached with a half-hearted salaam.

'Ah, so there you are, you old scoundrel!' exclaimed the Major, trying to sound friendly and jocular. 'More jungle than garden, from what I can see. You're getting too old for this sort of work, Dhuki. Time to retire! And where's the Memsahib?'

'Gone to the bazaar,' said Dhuki.

'And the boy?'

Dhuki shrugged. 'I have not seen the boy today, Sahib.'

'Damn!' said the Major. 'A fine homecoming, this is. Well, wake up the cook-boy and tell him to get some sodas.'

'Cook-boy's gone away,' said Dhuki.

'Well, I'll be double-damned,' said the Major.

The tonga went away, and the Major started pacing up and down the garden path. Then he saw Dhuki's unfinished work at the well. He grew purple in the face, strode across to the well, and started ranting at the old gardener.

Dhuki began making excuses. He said something about a shortage of bricks; the sickness of a niece; unsatisfactory cement; unfavourable weather; unfavourable gods. When none of this seemed to satisfy the Major, Dhuki began mumbling about something bubbling up from the bottom of the well, and pointed down into its depths. The Major stepped on to the low parapet and looked down. Dhuki kept pointing. The Major leant over a little.

Dhuki's hands moved swiftly, like a conjurer's making a pass. He did not actually push the Major. He appeared merely to tap him once on the bottom. I caught a glimpse of my stepfather's boots as he disappeared into the well. I couldn't help thinking of Alice in Wonderland, of Alice disappearing down the rabbit hole.

There was a tremendous splash, and the pigeons flew up, circling the well thrice before settling on the roof of the bungalow.

By lunch time—or tiffin, as we called it then—Dhuki had the well covered over with the wooden planks.

'The Major will be pleased,' said my mother, when she came home. 'It will be quite ready by evening, won't it, Dhuki?'

By evening, the well had been completely bricked over. It was the fastest bit of work Dhuki had ever done.

Over the next few weeks, my mother's concern changed to anxiety, her anxiety to melancholy, and her melancholy to resignation. By being gay and high-spirited myself, I hope I did something to cheer her up. She had written to the Colonel of the Regiment, and had been informed that the Major had gone home on leave a fortnight previously. Somewhere, in the vastness of India, the Major had disappeared.

It was easy enough to disappear and never be found. After

several months had passed without the Major turning up, it was presumed that one of the two things must have happened. Either he had been murdered on the train, and his corpse flung into a river; or, he had run away with a tribal girl and was living in some remote corner of the country.

Life had to carry on for the rest of us. The rains were over, and the guava season was approaching.

My mother was receiving visits from a colonel of His Majesty's 32nd Foot. He was an elderly, easy-going, seemingly absent-minded man, who didn't get in the way at all, but left slabs of chocolate lying around the house.

'A *good* Sahib,' observed Dhuki, as I stood beside him behind the bougainvillea, watching the colonel saunter up the verandah steps. 'See how well he wears his sola topi! It covers his head completely.'

'He's bald underneath,' I said.

'No matter. I think he will be all right.'

'And if he isn't,' I said, 'we can always open up the well again.'

Dhuki dropped the nozzle of the hosepipe, and water gushed out over our feet. But he recovered quickly, and taking me by the hand, led me across to the old well, now surmounted by a three-tiered cement platform which looked rather like a wedding cake.

'We must not forget our old well,' he said. 'Let us make it beautiful, Baba. Some flower pots, perhaps.'

And together we fetched pots, and decorated the covered well with ferns and geraniums. Everyone congratulated Dhuki on the fine job he'd done. My only regret was that the pigeons had gone away.

SIMPLY LIVING

These thoughts and observations were noted in my diaries through the 1980s, and may give readers some idea of the ups and downs, highs and lows, during a period when I was still trying to get established as an author.

March 1981

After a gap of twenty years, during which it was, to all practical purposes forgotten, *The Room on the Roof* (my first novel) gets reprinted in an edition for schools.

(This was significant, because it marked the beginning of my entry into the educational field. Gradually, over the years, more of my work became familiar to school children throughout the country.)

Stormy weather over Holi. Room flooded. Everyone taking turns with septic throats and fever. While in bed, read Stendhal's *The Red and the Black*. I seem to do my serious reading only when I'm sick.

Felt well enough to take a leisurely walk down the Tehri Road. Trees in new leaf. The fresh light green of the maples is very soothing.

I may not have contributed anything towards the progress of civilization, but neither have I robbed the world of anything. Not one tree or bush or bird. Even the spider on my wall is welcome to his (her) space. Provided he (she) stays on the wall and does not descend on my pillow.

April

Swifts are busy nesting in the roof and performing acrobatics outside my window. They do everything on the wing, it seems—including feeding and making love. Mating in midair must be quite a feat.

Someone complimented me because I was 'always smiling'. I thought better of him for the observation and invited him over. Flattery will get you anywhere!

(This is followed by a three-month gap in my diary, explained by my next entry.)

Shortage of cash. Muddle, muddle, toil and trouble. I don't see myself smiling.

Learn to zigzag. Try something different.

August

Kept up an article a day for over a month. Grub Street again!
DARE
WILL
KEEP SILENCE
These words helped Napoleon, but will they help me?
Try cursing!
I curse the block to money.
I curse the thing that takes all my effort away.

I curse all that would make me a slave.

I curse those who would harm my loved ones.

And now stop cursing and give thanks for all the good things you have enjoyed in life.

'We should not spoil what we have by desiring what we have not, but remember that what we have was the gift of fortune.'

(Epicurus)

◆

'We ought to have more sense, of course, than to try to touch a dream, or to reach that place which exists but in the glamour of a name.'

(H.M. Tomlinson, *Tide Marks*)

October

A good year for the cosmos flower. Banks of them everywhere. They like the day-long sun. Clean and fresh—my favourite flower *en-masse*.

But by itself, the wild commelina, sky-blue against dark green, always catches the heart.

A latent childhood remains tucked away in our subconscious. This I have tried to explore...

A...stretches out on the bench like a cat, and the setting sun is trapped in his eyes, golden brown, glowing like tiger's eyes. (Oddly enough, this beautiful youth grew up to become a very sombre-looking padre.)

December

A kiss in the dark—warm and soft and all-encompassing—the moment stayed with me for a long time.

Wrote a poem, 'Who kissed me in the dark?' but it could not do justice to the kiss. Tore it up!

On the night of the 7th, light snowfall. The earliest that I can remember it snowing in Landour. Early morning, the hillside looked very pretty, with a light mantle of snow covering trees, rusty roofs, vehicles at the bus stop—and concealing our garbage dump for a couple of hours, until it melted.

January 1982

Three days of wind, rain, sleet and snow. Flooded out of my bedroom. We convert dining room into dormitory. Everything is bearable except the wind, which cuts through these old houses like a knife—under the roof, through flimsy verandah enclosures and ill-fitting windows, bringing the icy rain with it.

Fed up with being stuck indoors. Walked up to Lal Tibba, in flurries of snow. Came back and wrote the story 'The Wind on Haunted Hill'.

I invoke Lakshmi, who shines like the full moon.

Her fame is all-pervading.

Her benevolent hands are like lotuses.

I take refuge in her lotus feet.

Let her destroy my poverty forever.

Goddess, I take shelter at your lotus feet.

February

My boyhood was difficult, but I had my dreams to sustain me. What does one dream about now?

But sometimes, when all else fails, a sense of humour comes to the rescue.

And the children (Raki, Muki, Dolly) bring me joy. All children do. Sometimes I think small children are the only sacred things left on this earth. Children and flowers.

Further blasts of wind and snow. In spite of the gloom, wrote a new essay.

March

Blizzard in the night. Over a foot of snow in the morning. And so it goes on...unprecedented for March. The Jupiter Effect? At least the snow prevents the roof from blowing away, as happened last year. Facing east (from where the wind blows) doesn't help. And it's such a rickety old house.

◆

Mid-March and the first warm breath of approaching summer. Risk a haircut. Ramkumar does his best to make me look like a 1930s film star. I suppose I ought to try another barber, but he's too nice. 'I look rather strange,' I said afterwards (like Wallace Beery in *Billy the Kid*). 'Don't worry,' he said. 'You'll get used to it.'

'Why don't you give me an Amitabh Bachchan haircut?'

'You'll need more hair for that,' he says.

◆

Bus goes down the mud, killing several passengers. Death moves about at random, without discriminating between the innocent and the evil, the poor and the rich. The only difference is that the poor usually handle it better.

Late March

The blackest clouds I've ever seen squatted over Mussoorie, and then it hailed marbles for half an hour. Nothing like a hailstorm to clear the sky. Even as I write, I see a rainbow forming.

And Goddess Lakshmi smiles on me. An unprecedented flow of cheques, mainly accrued royalties on 'Angry River' and 'The Blue Umbrella'. A welcome change from last year's shortages and difficulties.

Perfection

The smallest insect in the world is a sort of fairyfly and its body is only a fifth of a millimetre long. One can only just see it with the naked eye. Almost like a speck of dust, yet it has perfect little wings and little combs on its legs for preening itself.

Late April

Abominable cloud and chilly rain. But Usha brings bunches of wild roses and irises. And her own gentle smile.

Mid-May

Raki (after reading my biodata): 'Dada, you were born in 1934! And you are still here!' After a pause: 'You are very lucky.'

I guess I am, at that.

June

Did my sixth essay for *The Monitor* this year.

(Have written off and on, for *The Christian Science Monitor* of Boston from 1965 to 2002).

Wrote an article for a new magazine, *Keynote*, published in Bombay, and edited by Leela Naidu, Dom Moraes and David Davidar. It was to appear in the August issue. Now I'm told that the magazine has folded. (But David Davidar went on to bigger things with Penguin India!)

If at first you don't succeed, so much for skydiving.

July

Monsoon downpour. Bedroom wall crumbling. Landslide cuts off my walk down the Tehri road.

Usha: a complexion like apricot blossom seen through a mist.

September

Two dreams:

A constantly recurring dream or rather, nightmare—I am forced to stay longer than I had intended in a very expensive hotel and know that my funds are insufficient to meet the bill. Fortunately, I have always woken up before the bill is presented!

Possible interpretation: fear of insecurity. My own variation of the dream, common to many, of falling from a height but waking up before hitting the ground.

Another occasional dream: living in a house perched over a crumbling hillside. This one is not far removed from reality!

•

Glorious day. Walked up and around the hill, and got some of the cobwebs out of my head.

That man is strongest who stands alone!

Some epigrams (for future use).

A well-balanced person: someone with a chip on both shoulders.

Experience: the knowledge that enables you to recognize a mistake when you make it the second time.

Sympathy: what one woman offers another in exchange for details.

Worry: the interest paid on trouble before it becomes due.

October

Some disappointment, as usual in connection with films (the screenplay I wrote for someone who wanted to remake *Kim*), but if I were to let disappointments get me down, I'd have given up writing twenty-five years ago.

A walk in the twilight. Soothing. Watched the winter line from the top of the hill.

Raki first in school races.

Savitri (Dolly) completes two years. Bless her fat little toes.

Advice to myself: conserve energy. Talk less!

'Better to have people wondering why you don't speak than to have them wondering why you speak.' (Disraeli)

•

Wrote 'The Funeral'. One of my better stories, and thus, more difficult to place.

If death was a thing that money could buy,

The rich, they would live, and the poor, they would die.

In California, you can have your body frozen after death in the hope that a hundred years from now some scientist will come along and bring you to life again. You pay in advance, of course.

December

I never have much luck with films or filmmakers. Mr K.S. Varma, finally (after five years), completed his film of my story 'The Last Tiger', but could not find a distributor for it. I don't regret the small sum I received for the story. He ran out of money—and tigers!—and apparently went to heroic lengths to complete the film in the forests of Bihar and Orissa. He used a circus tiger for the more intimate scenes, but this tiger disappeared one day, along with one of the actors. Tom Alter played a shikari and went on to play other, equally hazardous roles: he's still around, the tiger having spared him, but the film was never seen (and hasn't been seen to this day).

◆

A last postcard from an old friend: 'Ruskin, dear friend— but you won't be, unless you keep your word about lunching with us on Xmas Day. PLEASE DO COME, both Kanshi and I need your presence. It will be a small party this time as most of our friends are either *hors-de-combat* or dead! Bring Rakesh and Mukesh. Please let me know. I have been in bed for two days with a chill. Please don't disappoint.

Love,
Winnie

(We did go to the Christmas party, but sadly, the chill became pneumonia and there were no more parties with Winnie and Kanshi, who were such good company. I still miss them.)

January 1984

To Maniram's home near Lal Tibba. He was brought up by his grandmother—his mother died when he was one. Keeps two calves, two cows (one brindled), and a pup of indeterminate breed. Made me swallow a glass of milk. Haven't touched milk for years, can't stand the stuff, but drank it so as not to hurt his feelings. (Mani and his Granny turned up in my children's story *Getting Granny's Glasses*.)

◆

On the 6th, it was bitterly cold and the snow came in through my bedroom roof. Not enough money to go away, but at least there's enough for wood and coal. I hate the cold—but the children seem to enjoy it. Raki, Muki and Dolly in constant high spirits.

◆

February

Two days and nights of blizzard—howling winds, hail, sleet, snow. Prem bravely goes out for coal and kerosene oil. Worst weather we've ever had up here. Sick of it.

◆

March

Peach, plum and apricot trees in blossom. Gentle weather at last. Schools reopen.

Sold German and Dutch translation rights in a couple of my children's books. I wish I could write something of lasting worth. I've done a few good stories but they are so easily lost in the mass of wordage that pours forth from the world's presses.

Here are some statistics which I got from the UK a couple of years ago:

There are over nine million books in the British Museum and they fill 86 miles of shelving.

There are over 50,000 living British authors. They don't get rich. The latest Society of Authors survey shows that only 55 per cent of those whose main occupation is writing earn over £700 a year.

Britain has 8,500 booksellers, as well as many other shops where books are sold.

The first book to be printed in Britain was *The Dictes and Sayings of the Philosophers,* which was translated and printed by William Caxton in 1477.

As many books were published in Britain between 1940 and 1980 as in the five centuries from Caxton's first book.

Who says the reading habit is dying?

◆

April

The 'adventure wind' of my boyhood—I felt it again today. Walked five miles to Suakholi, to look at an infinity of mountains.

The feeling of space—limitless space—can only be experienced by living in the mountains.

It is the emotional, the spiritual surge, that draws us back to the mountains again and again. It was not altogether a matter of mysticism or religion that prompted the ancients to believe that their gods dwelt in the high places of this earth. Those gods, by whatever name we know them, still dwell there. From time to time we would like to be near them, that we may know them and ourselves more intimately.

May

Completed my half-century and launched into my 51st year.

Fifty is a dangerous age for most men. Last year there was nothing to celebrate, and at the end of it my diary went into the dustbin. There was an abortive and unhappy love affair (dear reader, don't fall in love at fifty!), a crisis in the home (with Prem missing for weeks), conflicts with publishers, friends, myself. So skip being fifty. Become fifty-one as soon its possible; you will find yourself in calmer waters. If you fall in love at the age of fifty, inner turmoil and disappointment is almost guaranteed. Don't listen to what the wise men say about love. P.G. Wodehouse said the whole thing more succinctly: 'You know, the way love can change a fellow is really frightful to contemplate.' Especially when a fifty-year-old starts behaving like a sixteen-year-old!

Most of my month's earnings went to the dentist. And I notice he's wearing a new suit.

June

A name—a lovely face—turn back the years: 45 years to be exact, when I was a small boy in Jamnagar, where my father taught English to some of the younger princes and princesses—among them M—whose picture I still have in my album (taken by my father). She wrote to me after reading something I'd written, wanting to know if I was the same little boy, i.e., Mr Bond's mischievous son. I responded, of course. A link with my father is so rare; and besides, I had a crush on her. My first love! So long ago—but it seems like yesterday...

◆

Monsoon breaks.

Money-drought breaks.

And if there's a connection, may the rain gods be generous this year.

(The rest of the year's entries were fairly mundane, implying that life at Ivy Cottage, Landour, went on pretty smoothly. But the rain gods played a trick or two. Although they were fairly generous to begin with, the year ended with a drought, as my mid-December entry indicates: 'Dust covers everything, after nearly two and half months of dry weather. Clouds build up, but disperse.' Always receptive to Nature's unpredictability, I wrote my story *Dust on the Mountain*.)

1995

On the flyleaf of this year's diary are written two maxims: 'Pull your own strings' and 'Act impeccably'. I'm not sure that I did either with much success, but I did at least try. And trying is what it's all about...

January

My book of poems and prayers finally published by Thomson Press, *seven years* after acceptance. Received a copy. Hope it won't be the only one. Splendid illustrations by Suddha. (Shortly afterwards Thomson Press closed down their children's book division and my book vanished too!)

Can thought (consciousness) exist outside the body? Can it, be trained to do so? Can its existence continue after the body has gone? Does it *need* a body? (but without a body it would have nothing to do.)

Of course, thoughts can travel. But do they travel of their own volition, or because of the bodily energy that sustains them?

We have the wonders of clairvoyance, of presentiments, and premonitions in dreams. How to account for these?

Our thinking is conditioned by past experience (including the past experience of the human race), and so, as Bergson said: 'We think with only a small part of the past, but it is with our entire past, including the original bent of the soul, that we desire, will, and act.'

'The original bent of the soul...' I accept that man has a soul, or he would be incapable of compassion.

February

We move from mind to matter:

Tried a pizza—seemed to take an hour to travel down my gullet.

Two days later: Swiss cheese pie with Mrs Goel, who's Swiss—and more adventures of the digestive tract.

Next day: supper with the Deutschmanns from Australia. Australian pie.

Following day: rest and recovery. Then reverted to good old dal bhaat.

Accompanied N— to Dehra Dun and ended up paying for our lunch. The trouble with rich people is that they never seem to have any money on them. That's how they stay rich, I suppose.

March

Sold *A Crow for All Seasons* to the Children's Film Society for a small sum. They think it will make a good animated film. And so it will. But I'm pretty sure they won't make it. They have forgotten about the story they bought from me five years ago! (Neither film was ever made.)

April

The wind in the pines and deodars hums and moans, but in the chestnut, it rustles and chatters and makes cheerful conversation. The horse-chestnut in full leaf is a magnificent sight.

◆

Children down with mumps. I go clown with a viral fever for two days. Recover and write three articles. Hope for the best. It is not in mortals to *command* success.

◆

Men get their sensual natures from their mothers, their intellectual make-up from their fathers; women, the other way round. (Or so I'm told!)

June

Not many years ago, you had to walk for weeks to reach the pilgrim destinations—Badrinath, Gangotri, Kedarnath, Tungnath... Last week, within a few days, I covered them all, as most of them are now accessible by motorable road. I liked some of the smaller places, such as Nandprayag, which are still unspoilt. Otherwise, I'm afraid the dhaba-culture of urban India has followed the cars and buses into the mountains and up to the shrines.

July

The deodar (unlike the pine) is a hospitable tree. It allows other things to grow beneath it, and it tolerates growth upon its trunk and branches—moss, ferns, small plants. The tiny young cones are like blossoms on the dark green foliage at this time of the year.

◆

Slipped and cracked my head against the grid of a truck. Blood gushed forth, so I dashed across to Dr Joshi's little clinic and had three stitches and an anti-tetanus shot. Now you know why I don't travel well.

◆

M.C. Beautiful, seductive. 'She walks in beauty like the night...'

August

Endless rain. No sun for a week. But M.C. playful, loving. In good spirits, I wrote a funny story about cricket. I'd find it hard to write a serious story about cricket. The farcical element appeals to me more than the 'nobler' aspects of the game. Uncle Ken made more runs with his pads than with his bat. And out of every ten catches that came his way, he took one!

October

Paid rent in advance for next year; paid school fees to end of this year. Broke, but don't owe a paisa to a soul. Ice cream in town with Raki. Came home to find a couple of cheques waiting for me!

M.C. Quick as a vixen, but makes the chase worthwhile.

We walk in the wind and the rain. Exhilarating.

Frantic kisses.

Time to say goodbye!

When love is swiftly stolen,

It hasn't time to die.

When in love, I'm inspired to write bad verse.

Teilhard de Chardin said it better:

'Some day, after we have mastered the winds, the waves, the tides and gravity, we shall harness for God the energies of love. Then for the second time in the history of the world, man will have discovered fire.'

February 1986

Destiny is really the strength of our desires.

◆

Raki back from the village. I'm happy he has made himself popular there, adapted to both worlds, the comparative sophistication of Mussoorie and the simple earthiness of village Bachhanshu in the remoteness of Garhwal. Being able to get on with everyone, rich or poor, old or young, makes life so much easier. Or so I've found! My parents' broken marriage, father's early death, and the difficulties of adapting to my stepfather's home, resulted in my being something of a loner until I was thirty. Now I've become a family person without marrying. Selfish?

◆

Returned to two great comic novels—H.G. Wells's *History of Mr Polly* and George and Weedon Grossmith's *The Diary of Nobody*. *Polly* has some marvellous set-pieces, while *Nobody* never fails to make me laugh.

◆

M.C. returns with a spring in the Springtime. The same good nature and sense of humour.

> Three things in love the foolish will desire:
> Faith, constancy, and passion; but the wise
> Only an hour's happiness require
> And not to look into uncaring eyes.

(Kenneth Hopkins)

March

Getting Granny's Glasses received a nomination for the Carnegie Medal. *Cricket for the Crocodile* makes friends.

After a cold wet spell, Holi brings warmer days, ladybirds, new friends.

May

So now I'm 52. Time to pare life down to the basics of doing.
  a) what I have to do
  b) what I want to do
  Much prefer the latter.

June

Blood pressure up and down.

Writing for a living: it's a battlefield!

People do ask funny questions. Accosted on the road by a stranger, who proceeds to cross-examine me, starting with: 'Excuse me, are you a good writer?' For once, I'm stumped for an answer.

Muki's no better. Bangs my study door, sees me give a start, and says: 'This door makes a lot of noise, doesn't it?'

August

Thousands converge on the town from outlying villages, for a local festival. By late evening, scores of drunks staggering about on the road. A few fights, but largely good-natured.

The women dress very attractively and colourfully. But for most of the menfolk, the height of fashion appears to be a new pyjama-suit. But I'm a pyjama person myself. Pyjamas are comfortable, I write better wearing pyjamas!

September

Month began with a cheque that bounced. Refrained from checking my blood pressure.

◆

Monsoon growth at its peak. The ladies' slipper orchids are tailing off, but I noticed all the following wild flowers: balsam (two kinds), commelina, agrimony, wild geranium (very pretty), sprays of white flowers emanating from the wild ginger, the scarlet fruit of the cobra lily just forming tiny mushrooms set like pearls in a retaining wall; ferns still green, which means more rain to come; escaped dahlias everywhere; wild begonias and much else. The best time of year for wild flowers.

February 1987

Home again, after five days in hospital with bleeding ulcers. Loving care from Prem. Support from Ganesh and others. Nurse Nirmala very caring. I prefer nurses to doctors.

Milk, hateful milk!

After a week, back in hospital. Must have been all that milk. Or maybe Nurse Nirmala!

March

To Delhi for a check-up. Public gardens ablaze with flowers. Felt much better.

'A merry heart does good like a medicine, but a broken spirit dries the bones.'

'He who tenderly brings up his servant from a child, shall have him become his son at the end.'

(Book of Proverbs)

May

Lines for future use:

Lunch (at my convent school) was boiled mutton and overcooked pumpkin, which made death lose some of its sting.

Pictures on the wall are not just something to look at. After a time, they become company.

Another bus accident, and a curious crowd gathered with disaster-inspired speed.

He (Upendra) has a bonfire of a laugh.

(Forgot to use these lines, so here they are!)

May

Ordered a birthday cake, but it failed to arrive. Sometimes I think inertia is the greatest force in the world.

Wrote a ghost story, something I enjoy doing from time to time, although I must admit that, try as I might, I have yet to encounter a supernatural being. Unless you can count dreams as being supernatural experiences.

August

After the drought, the deluge.

Landslide near the house. It rumbled away all night and I kept getting up to see how close it was getting to us. About twenty feet away. The house is none too stable, badly in need of repairs. In fact, it looks a bit like the Lucknow Residency after the rebels had finished shelling it.

(It did, however, survive the landslide, although the retaining wall above our flat collapsed, filling the sitting-room with rubble.)

November

To Delhi, to receive a generous award from Indian Council for Child Education. Presented to me by the Vice President of India. Got back to my host's home to discover that the envelope contained another awardee's cheque. He was due to leave for Ahmedabad by train. Rushed to railway station, to find him on the platform studying my cheque which he had just discovered in his pocket. Exchanged cheques. All's well that ends well.

A Delhi Visit

A long day's taxi journey to Delhi. It gets tiring towards the end, but I have always found the road journey interesting and at times quite enchanting—especially the rural scene from outside Dehradun, through Roorkee and various small wayside towns, up to Muzaffarnagar and the outskirts of Meerut: the sugar-cane being harvested and taken to the sugar factories (by cart or truck); the fruit on sale everywhere (right now, it's the season for bananas and 'chakotra' lemons); children bathing in small canals; the serenity of mango groves...

Of course, there's the other side to all this—the litter that accumulates wherever there are large centres of population; the blaring of horns; loudspeakers here and there. It's all part of the picture. But the picture as a whole is a fascinating one, and the colours can't be matched anywhere else.

Marigolds blaze in the sun. Yes, whole fields of them, for they are much in demand on all sorts of ceremonial occasions: marriages, temple pujas, and garlands for dignitaries—making the humble marigold a good cash crop.

And not so humble after all. For although the rose may

still be the queen of flowers, and the jasmine the princess of fragrance, the marigold holds its own through sheer sturdiness, colour and cheerfulness. It is a cheerful flower, no doubt about that—brightening up winter days, often when there is little else in bloom. It doesn't really have a fragrance—simply an acid odour, not to everyone's liking—but it has a wonderful range of colour, from lower yellow to deep orange to golden bronze, especially among the giant varieties in the hills.

Otherwise this is not a great month for flowers, although at the India International Centre (IIC) in Delhi, where I am staying, there is a pretty tree with fragile pink flowers—the Chorisia speciosa, each bloom having five large pink petals, with long pistula.

THE FLUTE PLAYER

Down the main road passed big yellow buses, cars, pony-drawn tongas, motorcycles and bullock carts. This steady flow of traffic seemed, somehow, to form a barrier between the city on one side of the Trunk Road, and the distant sleepy villages on the other. It seemed to cut India in half—the India Kamla knew slightly, and the India she had never seen.

Kamla's grandmother lived on the outskirts of the city of Jaipur, and just across the road from the house there were fields and villages stretching away for hundreds of miles. But Kamla had never been across the main road. This separated the busy city from the flat green plains stretching endlessly towards the horizon.

Kamla was used to city life. In England, it was London and Manchester. In India, it was Delhi and Jaipur. Rainy Manchester was, of course, different in many ways from sun-drenched Jaipur, and Indian cities had stronger smells and more vibrant colours than their English counterparts. Nevertheless, they had much in common: busy people always on the move, money constantly changing hands, buses to catch, schools to attend, parties to go to, TV to watch. Kamla had seen very little of the English countryside, even less of India outside the cities.

Her parents lived in Manchester where her father was a doctor in a large hospital. She went to school in England. But this year, during the summer holidays, she had come to India to stay with her grandmother. Apart from a maidservant and a grizzled old nightwatchman, Grandmother lived quite alone in a small house on the outskirts of Jaipur. During the winter months, Jaipur's climate was cool and bracing but in the summer, a fierce sun poured down upon the city from a cloudless sky.

None of the other city children ventured across the main road into the fields of millet, wheat and cotton, but Kamla was determined to visit the fields before she returned to England. From the flat roof of the house, she could see them stretching away for miles, the ripening wheat swaying in the hot wind. Finally, when there were only two days left before she went to Delhi to board a plane for London, she made up her mind and crossed the main road.

She did this in the afternoon, when Grandmother was asleep and the servants were in the bazaar. She slipped out of the back door and her slippers kicked up the dust as she ran down the path to the main road. A bus roared past and more dust rose from the road and swirled about her. Kamla ran through the dust, past the jacaranda trees that lined the road, and into the fields.

Suddenly, the world became an enormous place, bigger and more varied than it had seemed from the air, also mysterious and exciting—and just a little frightening.

The sea of wheat stretched away till it merged with the hot blinding blue of the sky. Far to her left were a few trees and the low white huts of a village. To her right lay hollow pits of red dust and a blackened chimney where bricks used to be made. In front, some distance away, Kamla could see a camel moving round a well, drawing up water for the fields. She set out in the direction of the camel.

Her grandmother had told her not to wander off on her own in the city; but this wasn't the city, and as far as she knew, camels did not attack people.

It took her a long time to get to the camel. It was about half a mile away, though it seemed much nearer. And when Kamla reached it, she was surprised to find that there was no one else in sight. The camel was turning the wheel by itself, moving round and round the well, while the water kept gushing up in little trays to run down the channels into the fields. The camel took no notice of Kamla, did not look at her even once, just carried on about its business.

There must be someone here, thought Kamla, walking towards a mango tree that grew a few yards away. Ripe mangoes dangled like globules of gold from its branches. Under the tree, fast asleep, was a boy.

All he wore was a pair of dirty white shorts. His body had been burnt dark by the sun; his hair was tousled, his feet chalky with dust. In the palm of his outstretched hand was a flute. He was a thin boy, with long bony legs, but Kamla felt that he was strong too, for his body was hard and wiry.

Kamla came nearer to the sleeping boy, peering at him with some curiosity, for she had not seen a village boy before. Her shadow fell across his face. The coming of the shadow woke the boy. He opened his eyes and stared at Kamla. When she did not say anything, he sat up, his head a little to one side, his hands clasping his knees, and stared at her.

'Who are you?' he asked a little gruffly. He was not used to waking up and finding strange girls staring at him.

'I'm Kamla. I've come from England, but I'm really from India. I mean I've come home to India, but I'm really from

England.' This was getting to be rather confusing, so she countered with an abrupt, 'Who are you?'

'I'm the strongest boy in the village,' said the boy, deciding to assert himself without any more ado. 'My name is Romi. I can wrestle and swim and climb any tree.'

'And do you sleep a lot?' asked Kamla innocently.

Romi scratched his head and grinned.

'I must look after the camel,' he said. 'It is no use staying awake for the camel. It keeps going round the well until it is tired, and then it stops. When it has rested, it starts going round again. It can carry on like that all day. But it eats a lot.'

Mention of the camel's food reminded Romi that he was hungry. He was growing fast these days and was nearly always hungry. There were some mangoes lying beside him, and he offered one to Kamla. They were silent for a few minutes. You cannot suck mangoes and talk at the same time. After they had finished, they washed their hands in the water from one of the trays.

'There are parrots in the tree,' said Kamla, noticing three or four green parrots conducting a noisy meeting in the topmost branches. They reminded her a bit of a pop group she had seen and heard at home.

'They spoil most of the mangoes,' said Romi.

He flung a stone at them, missed, but they took off with squawks of protest, flashes of green and gold wheeling in the sunshine.

'Where do you swim?' asked Kamla. 'Down in the well?'

'Of course not. I'm not a frog. There is a canal not far from here. Come, I will show you!'

As they crossed the fields, a pair of blue jays flew out of a bush, rockets of bright blue that dipped and swerved, rising and falling as they chased each other.

Remembering a story that Grandmother had told her, Kamla said, 'They are sacred birds, aren't they? Because of their blue throats.' She told him the story of the God Shiva having a blue throat because he had swallowed a poison that would have destroyed the world; he had kept the poison in his throat and would not let it go further. 'And so his throat is blue, like the blue jay's.'

Romi liked this story. His respect for Kamla greatly increased. But he was not to be outdone, and when a small grey squirrel dashed across the path he told her that squirrels, too, were sacred. Krishna, the god who had been born into a farmer's family like Romi's, had been fond of squirrels and would take them in his arms and stroke them. 'That is why squirrels have four dark lines down their backs,' said Romi. 'Krishna was very dark, as dark as I am, and the stripes are the marks of his fingers.'

'Can you catch a squirrel?' asked Kamla.

'No, they are too quick. But I caught a snake once. I caught it by its tail and dropped it in the old well. That well is full of snakes. Whenever we catch one, instead of killing it, we drop it in the well! They can't get out.'

Kamla shuddered at the thought of all those snakes swimming and wriggling about at the bottom of the deep well. She wasn't sure that she wanted to return to the well with him. But she forgot about the snakes when they reached the canal.

It was a small canal, about ten metres wide, and only waist-deep in the middle, but it was very muddy at the bottom. She had never seen such a muddy stream in her life.

'Would you like to get in?' asked Romi.

'No,' said Kamla. 'You get in.'

Romi was only too ready to show off his tricks in the water. His toes took a firm hold on the grassy bank, the muscles of his calves tensed, and he dived into the water with a loud splash, landing rather awkwardly on his belly. It was a poor dive, but Kamla was impressed.

Romi swam across to the opposite bank and then back again. When he climbed out of the water, he was covered with mud. It made him look quite fierce. 'Come on in,' he invited. 'It's not deep.'

'It's dirty,' said Kamla, but felt tempted all the same.

'It's only mud,' said Romi. 'There's nothing wrong with mud. Camels like mud. Buffaloes love mud.'

'I'm not a camel—or a buffalo.'

'All right. You don't have to go right in, just walk along the sides of the channel.'

After a moment's hesitation, Kamla slipped her feet out of her slippers, and crept cautiously down the slope till her feet were in the water. She went no further, but even so, some of the muddy water splashed on to her clean white skirt. What would she tell Grandmother? Her feet sank into the soft mud and she gave a little squeal as the water reached her knees. It was with some difficulty that she got each foot out of the sticky mud.

Romi took her by the hand, and they went stumbling along the side of the channel while little fish swam in and out of their legs, and a heron, one foot raised, waited until they had passed before snapping a fish out of the water. The little fish glistened in the sun before it disappeared down the heron's throat.

Romi gave a sudden exclamation and came to a stop. Kamla held on to him for support.

'What is it?' she asked, a little nervously.

'It's a tortoise,' said Romi. 'Can you see it?'

He pointed to the bank of the canal, and there, lying quite still, was a small tortoise. Romi scrambled up the bank and, before Kamla could stop him, had picked up the tortoise. As soon as he touched it, the animal's head and legs disappeared into its shell. Romi turned it over, but from behind the breastplate only the head and a spiky tail were visible.

'Look!' exclaimed Kamla, pointing to the ground where the tortoise had been lying. 'What's in that hole?'

They peered into the hole. It was about half a metre deep, and at the bottom were five or six white eggs, a little smaller than a hen's eggs.

'Put it back,' said Kamla. 'It was sitting on its eggs.'

Romi shrugged and dropped the tortoise back on its hole. It peeped out from behind its shell, saw the children were still present, and retreated into its shell again.

'I must go,' said Kamla. 'It's getting late. Granny will wonder where I have gone.'

They walked back to the mango tree, and washed their hands and feet in the cool clear water from the well; but only after Romi had assured Kamla that there weren't any snakes in the well—he had been talking about an old disused well on the far side of the village. Kamla told Romi she would take him to her house one day, but it would have to be next year, or perhaps the year after, when she came to India again.

'Is it very far, where you are going?' asked Romi.

'Yes, England is across the seas. I have to go back to my parents. And my school is there, too. But I will take the plane from Delhi. Have you ever been to Delhi?'

'I have not been further than Jaipur,' said Romi. 'What is England like? Are there canals to swim in?'

'You can swim in the sea. Lots of people go swimming in the sea. But it's too cold most of the year. Where I live, there are shops and cinemas and places where you can eat anything you like. And people from all over the world come to live there. You can see red faces, brown faces, black faces, white faces!'

'I saw a red face once,' said Romi. 'He came to the village to take pictures. He took one of me sitting on the camel. He said he would send me the picture, but it never came.'

Kamla noticed the flute lying on the grass. 'Is it your flute?' she asked.

'Yes,' said Romi. 'It is an old flute. But the old ones are best. I found it lying in a field last year. Perhaps it was the God Krishna's! He was always playing the flute.'

'And who taught you to play it?'

'Nobody. I learnt by myself. Shall I play it for you?'

Kamla nodded, and they sat down on the grass, leaning against the trunk of the mango tree, and Romi put the flute to his lips and began to play.

It was a slow, sweet tune, a little sad, a little happy, and the notes were taken up by the breeze and carried across the fields. There was no one to hear the music except the birds and the camel, and Kamla. Whether the camel liked it or not, we shall never know; it just kept going round and round the well, drawing up water for the fields. And whether the birds liked it or not, we cannot say, although it is true that they were all suddenly silent when Romi began to play. But Kamla was charmed by the music, and she watched Romi while he played, and the boy smiled at her with his eyes and ran his fingers along the flute. When he stopped playing, everything was still, everything silent, except for the soft wind sighing in the wheat and the gurgle of water coming up from the well.

Kamla stood up to leave.

'When will you come again?' asked Romi.

'I will try to come next year,' said Kamla.

'That is a long time. By then you will be quite old. You may not want to come.'

'I will come,' said Kamla.

'Promise?'

'Promise.'

Romi put the flute in her hands and said, 'You keep it. I can get another one.'

'But I don't know how to play it,' said Kamla.

'It will play by itself,' said Romi.

She took the flute and put it to her lips and blew on it, producing a squeaky little note that startled a lone parrot out of the mango tree. Romi laughed, and while he was laughing, Kamla turned and ran down the path through the fields. And when she had gone some distance, she turned and waved to Romi with the flute. He stood near the well and waved back at her.

Cupping his hands to his mouth, he shouted across the fields, 'Don't forget to come next year!'

And Kamla called back, 'I won't forget.' But her voice was faint, and the breeze blew the words away and Romi did not hear them.

Was England home? wondered Kamla. Or was this Indian city home? Or was her true home in that other India, across the busy Trunk Road? Perhaps she would find out one day.

Romi watched her until she was just a speck in the distance, and then he turned and shouted at the camel, telling it to move faster. But the camel did not even glance at him; it just carried on as before, as India has carried on for thousands of years, round and round and round the well, while the water gurgled and splashed over the smooth stones.